BOUNTY HUNTER'S REVENGE

With two years in jail behind him, Adam Milton rode into Cotterton in search of a job. Finding work as bodyguard to Miss Chambers, owner of the Big C ranch, Milton is dragged into the feud between her and ranch owner Trimble. But when Miss Chambers is shot he unhesitatingly steps into the vendetta between the two ranches. The ensuing violence leaves a trail of corpses and poses the question: will Milton become one of them?

Thi'
la'

●

●

RON WATKINS

BOUNTY HUNTER'S REVENGE

Complete and Unabridged

LINFORD
Leicester

First published in Great Britain in 2005 by
Robert Hale Limited
London

First Linford Edition
published 2006
by arrangement with
Robert Hale Limited
London

The moral right of the author
has been asserted

British Library CIP Data

Watkins, Ron, *1930 –*
    Bounty hunter's revenge.—Large print ed.—
Linford western library
    1. Western stories
    2. Large type books
    I. Title
    823.9'14 [F]

ISBN 1–84617–512–7

Published by
F. A. Thorpe (Publishing)
Anstey, Leicestershire

Set by Words & Graphics Ltd.
Anstey, Leicestershire
Printed and bound in Great Britain by
T. J. International Ltd., Padstow, Cornwall

This book is printed on acid-free paper

For my grand-daughter,
Tania Sparks

1

'What does a feller have to do to get a job around here?'

The question was directed at the barman of the Golden Eye saloon. The stranger who had posed the question could be a cowboy, the barman decided. When he had handed him his beer he had instinctively glanced at the stranger's hands. They were the hands of a manual worker rather than of a gambler or a professional man. The one thing that puzzled the barman was that although the stranger was dressed like a cowboy and had the hands of a cowboy, he didn't have the expected weather-beaten face of a cowboy. He was tall with a pale face — not the face of a man who was used to spending hours each day in the saddle out in all weathers.

'Most men who are looking for work

in Cotterton go to see Lady Iron Pants,' replied the barman.

'I asked a civil question, and I expect a civil answer.'

Although the remark was delivered in an apparent casual manner there was the hint of a threat in the stranger's reply which immediately put the barman on his guard. Why was the stranger so touchy?

'It's true. The person who owns most of the land around Cotterton is a Miss Chambers. Everybody knows her as Lady Iron Pants — although not to her face, of course.'

To the barman's relief the stranger smiled.

'So a woman owns most of the land around here? How old is she?'

'I'm not sure.' The barman scratched his head. 'About thirty I would guess.'

'So how did she become the number one lady around here?'

'She inherited it from her father. He died a few years back.'

The stranger finished his beer.

'How do I find her ranch?'

The barman gave him instructions. 'It's about a couple of miles out of town,' he added.

Half an hour later the stranger turned off the road to follow the signpost which said: CHAMBERS RANCH. He had ridden for a couple of miles before he came to the ranch. As he rode towards it he saw that he was being watched by a couple of guards who were stationed near the gate which led to the house.

Both men carried guns, a point which the stranger observed as he rode slowly up to them.

'Right, that's far enough,' said one of the guards. 'Just state your business, stranger.'

'I'm looking for work. I was told that I might find it here.'

'Who told you?' enquired the other guard.

'The barman in the Golden Eye saloon. I don't know his name.'

'Sol James. He's sent a few guys here.'

'You'd better come in to see Miss Chambers,' stated the other. 'By the way, what's your name?'

'Milton.'

'All right, Milton, follow me.'

He dismounted, tied his horse to the rail and followed the guard. The house was quite spacious with carpet on the floor of the hall where he would have expected bare boards. The guard stopped outside one of the rooms on the left and knocked.

'Come in,' said a female voice.

The owner of the voice was seated behind a large mahogany desk. She had a round face topped by short black hair, but she was on the right side of plain.

'This feller, Milton, is looking for a job, Miss Chambers,' said the guard, deferentially.

'All right, Calan, leave us.'

She waited until the door was closed behind the guard. Milton was aware of her studying him. In fact she stared at him for several seconds before delivering the opening gambit.

'Why do you want a job, Milton?'

'I've been a member of a chain-gang for the past two years. I was released on a pardon a few weeks back. I can show you the pardon if you want to see it.'

There was no mistaking the bitterness in his voice.

'Show me your hands.'

He showed her the hands which bore the hall marks of hard manual work. Then without a word he rolled up his left sleeve. There was a number grafted there.

'They branded us like cattle.'

The bitterness was again apparent. There was a flicker of emotion on her face. Sympathy?

'I can't employ you until I get the full story about why you were jailed in the first place.'

'I was a bounty hunter. I wanted to save up enough money to buy a farm and raise horses. I caught a few men. I had to kill a couple of them. I fell foul of a sheriff in Sula. He claimed that he should have had the reward for the men I had caught. When I argued with him, he put me in jail. He invented a charge that I had been a member of the gang who had held up the bank. The judge believed him. I was sentenced to five years' hard labour. A few months ago the leader of the gang was caught. He stated that I wasn't a member of his gang. The sheriff then admitted that he had made a mistake. Do you want to see the pardon?' He reached inside his pocket.

She waved a dismissive hand.

'No, I believe you.'

'So that's why I'm looking for a job.'

She subjected him to a long scrutiny. At last she seemed to make up her mind.

'You can use a gun, Milton?'

'I was in a couple of gun fights with the guys who were wanted by the law. I managed to survive,' he said, with a twisted grin.

'So I see. Well, anyhow I need a bodyguard. The person who had the job before came to an unfortunate end last week. I need a replacement.'

'He died?'

'Yes, he was shot. The sheriff is investigating it. I haven't much faith in him.'

'I know the feeling.'

For the first time she smiled. It changed her face from that of a hard-headed business woman to an attractive one.

'Do you want the job?'

'Sure. How much does it pay?'

'Twenty dollars a week and all found.'

'I'll take it.'

2

Although to all appearances Milton was accepted by the other cowboys of the Big C ranch, he sensed the undercurrent of resentment towards him. Here he was, a complete stranger, who had been chosen for one of the plum jobs on the ranch. Several of the cowboys had eyed the post of bodyguard to Lady Iron Pants with expectation. Some of them had worked several years on the ranch and had seen it as their main chance of promotion — not to mention the extra money which would go with it.

Chief among those who were disgruntled about the appointment were the two guards Milton had met on the gate, Calan and Mars.

'One of us should have had the job,' said Calan, the following day when they were at their usual position guarding the gate.

'I don't see how she came to appoint him,' stated Mars. Both were hard men who had spent years riding the range.

'He is a big man,' ventured Calan. He himself was rather short, and often felt that his lack of height had been a handicap in his life.

'So what?' said Mars, scornfully. Although he was not quite as tall as Milton, he almost reached six feet.

'She couldn't have known anything about him,' said Calan.

'He hasn't spent most of his life out on the range. He's too pale for that,' stated the other.

'Where is he now?' demanded Calan.

'He's taken my lady into town. She goes shopping while he sits in the coffee house drinking coffee.'

'One of us should have had that job,' said Calan, morosely.

'I wonder where he came from?' asked Mars, thoughtfully.

'We'll probably never find out.'

'There might be a clue though.'

'What do you mean?'

'He's got some belongings which he keeps rolled up at the foot of his bed in the bunkhouse. Maybe it would be a good idea to have a look at them.'

His companion's expression changed. A glimmer of hope spread across his face.

'Yes, it wouldn't do any harm to find out what he was doing before he came here.'

'The boys are all out on the range. Now is your chance to search his belongings.'

'Why me?'

'One of us has to stay here. And it was my idea.'

'All right. But if they come back you've got to warn me.'

'They won't come back,' said Mars, positively. 'They've barely been gone an hour.'

Calan hurried over to the bunkhouse. He knew Milton's bed — it was the one on the end. He walked down between the beds until he came to it. He lifted up the straw mattress and looked underneath. There was a rolled-up oilskin which was tied at the end. Calan untied the knots gingerly.

He found that he was staring at several posters — the kind that are displayed in a sheriff's office. They offered rewards ranging from fifty dollars to 200 dollars for the capture of the outlaw depicted on the poster. The other item in the bundle was an official-looking document with the county crest stamped in the corner. The light in the bunkhouse was too weak, also, if truth were told, his reading ability was quite poor. He hastily rolled up the posters and put them back in the oilskin. He was about to put them back where he had found them when he changed his mind — he tied them up more or less exactly as he had found them. The official document he slipped into his pocket.

Two minutes later he appeared by Mars's side.

'Well? What did you find?' the

question was asked eagerly.

'He had some posters. They were the kind that you see in a sheriff's office.'

Mars digested the information.

'Do you think he was a sheriff?'

'I dunno. But there was also this document.'

Calan proudly unrolled the official paper. He handed it to his companion.

'It's from the county court,' Mars announced. There was a pause while he digested some of the paragraphs.

'What does the court have to say?' demanded Calan, impatiently.

Mars replied slowly: 'It says that he has been pardoned for having been a member of the Smollet gang. There's a lot of legal terms, but that's the gist of it. It says that he's got an unconditional pardon.'

'So he was a member of a gang of outlaws?' demanded Calan, excitedly.

'It looks like it.' His companion was studying the document again. 'It says that his five-year sentence has been rescinded — whatever that may mean.'

'So he was sentenced to five years in prison, but he was released before his time was up?'

'That's about it.'

'So he was an outlaw?'

'So it would seem.'

'I wonder if my lady knows about this?'

They stared at each other with the light of hope on their faces. Whereas until now it had seemed that Milton's appointment had effectively closed the door on their own chances of promotion, maybe the new knowledge which they had gleaned had provided them with a way to open it again.

3

The following morning Miss Chambers summoned Milton to her study early. Instead of telling him to sit down, as had been customary in the past few days, she left him standing.

'I believe you've been less than honest with me, Milton,' she said, coldly.

'I don't understand.'

'I've been privy to certain information — don't ask me how I received it, that shows you were a member of a gang of outlaws. Not that you were set up as you stated.'

Milton turned white with anger. He clenched his fists.

'The bastards. I thought somebody had gone through my belongings.'

She waved a dismissive hand.

'Never mind about that. What have you got to say for yourself?'

'What I told you is true. I'll get the pardon to prove it.'

She waited impatiently for his return. She was tapping the desk with her fingers when he came back. He handed her the document without a word.

She studied it for several minutes. At last she said: 'This seems quite clear. It states that you were inadvertently charged with being a member of the gang.'

'The two clowns at the gate don't know the meaning of the word 'inadvertently',' snapped Milton.

'So it seems.' She leaned back in her chair and studied him.

'What are you going to do about it?'

'I'm going to sack them.'

'Isn't it a bit drastic?'

'Why? They obviously didn't steal anything from your belongings. But they have shown they are basically dishonest. They also made a fool of me by making me accuse you. I don't take kindly to being made a fool of.'

Half an hour later, having packed

their belongings, Calan and Mars rode slowly away from the ranch.

'The bastard,' stated Mars, venomously.

'The swine,' said Calan.

'He must have poisoned her mind against us.'

'I've worked ten years on the ranch. I worked for her father.'

'So did I. Though I've only worked about four years.'

'If he thinks he's going to get away with this, then he's got another think coming. What are we going to do now?' demanded Calan.

'We've only got one choice.'

'What's that?'

'We'll have to go to work for the Tall T.'

'But that will mean working for Trimble,' protested Calan.

'Well, we haven't any choice,' said Mars, irritably. 'He's the only other big rancher in Cotterton. He's bound to be able to have jobs for us — especially at this time of the year.'

'I suppose you're right. But you know what it will mean.'

'Yes, it will mean spending six hours in the saddle instead of having an easy job at the gate.'

Half an hour later the two were in the Golden Eye saloon. They had decided to have a few drinks to help to forget the treatment they had received.

'It's unusual to see you two guys in here in the morning,' observed the barman, Sol James.

'We wouldn't be here if it wasn't for that bastard,' said Mars.

'It's all the fault of the swine,' Calan concurred.

'At a guess I'd say that someone has upset the two of you,' said Sol, drily.

'You wouldn't have to go far to guess his name since he came here asking for a job last week,' said Mars.

Sol scratched his head. It was an action which seemed to help his thought processes since in a few moments he exclaimed: 'The tall feller. The pale-faced guy?'

'That's him. Milton.' Mars spat into a nearby spittoon.

'He's really upset you?' Sol was fishing for information. He was a collector of any juicy bits of tittle-tattle which he would pass on to his wife who ran the kitchen in the saloon.

'Upset us? The bastard only got us the sack, didn't he?'

'But you two have been working for the Chambers family for years.'

'I've been working for ten years,' said Calan. 'Mars, here, has been working for four.'

'So how did you two come to get the sack?'

'It's a long story,' said Mars, who didn't see why he should feed the nosy barman's desire for titbits of gossip.

It was when they were on the fourth drink and the future seemed to be less gloomy than when they had come into the saloon that Mars came up with a startling suggestion.

'We'll tell Mr Trimble that we're willing to help him to kill Milton.'

'Wh — at?' Calan almost choked on his beer.

'We want to get rid of Milton, don't we? That way we should get our jobs back.'

'Ye - es.'

'Well, we've often talked about who got rid of the previous bodyguard, Rand. We agreed it must be one of Trimble's gunmen.'

'Yes.' Now he could see where his friend's reasoning was leading, he could regard his conclusion without panic.

'So we go to Trimble and tell him that we're willing to help him to get rid of Milton. We've got the inside information. We'll be able to tell him the best way to kill Milton.'

'I don't want anything to do with the killing.' Panic was beginning to set in again.

'We won't have to do anything about the killing,' said Mars, scornfully. 'Rand was killed when he was on his way to Cotterton, wasn't he?'

'Yes.'

19

'So we tell Trimble about Milton's movements and he will know when will be the best time to kill him.'

'But Milton doesn't come into Cotterton. At least he hasn't so far.'

'Not on his own, he doesn't. But he comes into town with Miss Chambers. She rides in the buggy and he rides his horse. It will be the perfect way for one of Trimble's gunmen to get rid of him.'

'Ye - es, I suppose so,' said a thoughtful Calan.

Sol came over to where they were leaning against the bar.

'Do you two want refills?' he demanded.

'No, thanks,' said Mars, as he headed for the door. 'We've got some business to attend to.'

'They seem happier than when they came in,' Sol observed to one of the regulars who was standing nearby.

'It can't be anything to do with the beer,' came the reply. 'This tastes like gnat's pee.'

4

On the Trimble ranch four men were gathered in Mr Trimble's study. Three of them were standing while Mr Trimble was seated behind his desk. The study was not as tastefully furnished as Erica's study. The only items of furniture were the old wooden desk behind which the old man was sitting, and an equally old drinks cabinet. Whereas Erica's study had a thick carpet on the floor, this one had a bare floor. The numerous burn marks testified to the number of cigarettes and cigars which had been stubbed out on it.

'You say Miss Chambers and her bodyguard have caught the stage?'

The remark was directed to one of his two sons. His name was Lugg and probably his one claim to fame was that in the school, which he attended until he was twelve, he had regularly achieved the distinction of being the bottom of the class.

'Yes, Pa. The feller who keeps the livery stable told me. They left the buggy there.'

'Did he know where she was heading for?'

'He said that Miss Chambers said they were going to Chicago.'

'That's a long way away.' The observation came from Lugg's twin brother, Miles. Although they were twins they didn't resemble each other, except that they both had the same shade of red hair. Lugg was a large, lumbering specimen, while Miles was slim. However the brains had been shared out equally between them, since Miles was no quicker in thought than his brother.

'If they're going to Chicago, that means they must be catching the train from Adamsville,' said their father, thoughtfully. Although he was in his seventies, there was nothing wrong with his brain. He often complained that during his life he had had to do the thinking for the three of them.

'So there'll be no chance of killing the bodyguard for a few days,' said the other person in the study. He was dressed in black. He was in his early thirties and apart from the fact that he wore two guns, there was nothing remarkable about his thin features.

'On the other hand it will give you an ideal opportunity, Simms,' said Trimble.

'How can he shoot the bodyguard if we don't know when he'll be coming back?' demanded Lugg.

'Work it out, son,' said his father. 'How many times a week does the stage arrive in town?'

'Twice,' said Lugg, unhesitatingly.

'On what days?'

'Tuesdays and Fridays.'

'What day did Miss Chambers and her bodyguard go on the stage?'

Lugg shifted uncomfortably. He wasn't sure where this questioning was leading.

'Yesterday, Pa. Friday.'

'That's right, son. Friday. They would have gone to Adamsville. They would have to have stopped overnight there. So they would be catching the train on what day?'

'Saturday,' stated Lugg, with some relief, having assumed that the questions were over.

'So they would get into Chicago on Saturday night. Now, after Saturday we get . . . ?'

'Sunday.' This time the answer came from Miles.

'And on Sunday what happens?' pursued their father, relentlessly.

'Nothing. Everything is shut,' stated Miles.

'Exactly.' His father regarded his son with something approaching approbation.

'Now we'll assume that Miss Chambers has some specific reason for going to Chicago — say to see a lawyer.'

'There are two lawyers in Cotterton,' put in Lugg.

'Yes, but everybody knows one of them is crooked. Anyhow maybe Miss Chambers has some other reason for going to Chicago. The point is that she cannot spend any time in the town if she intends coming back on the stage on Tuesday. She'd barely have an hour before she would have to catch the train back to Adamsville.'

'She might conclude her business in an hour,' suggested Simms.

'I don't think so. Miss Chambers is a woman, even though she's always dressed as a man. She won't be able to resist seeing some of the shops in Chicago, having come all that way.'

'You're probably right,' stated Simms.

'So we know exactly when she'll be coming back — on the stage next Friday. They'll collect the buggy. They'll be tired after their long journey. The bodyguard won't be watching out for an ambush. You pick your spot and kill him.'

The old man might have been discussing shooting a lame steer.

'I didn't have much trouble getting rid of Rand,' stated Simms. 'This new guy shouldn't be any problem either.'

'Then it won't be long until we take over the Big C ranch, Pa,' said Lugg, excitedly.

'All in good time,' said the old man.

5

Milton and Erica's journey to Chicago was uneventful. The journey on the stage to Adamsville was a long and tedious one. Apart from the two stops there was little conversation between them. Indeed there was hardly any conversation between the other six passengers on the stage either. The journey didn't seem conducive to conversation. Possibly because they were all crammed in such a small space.

On one occasion one of the ladies on the stage did try to open up a conversation.

'Are you young couple going all the way to Adamsville?'

It took Milton a second or two to realize that the woman opposite was talking to them. Then it dawned on him that they were the two youngest travellers on the stage.

'Yes, we are,' replied Erica, shortly.

'We're going all the way to Chicago,' stated the woman. She included her husband in the remark even though he was fast asleep and snoring lightly.

'So are we,' said Erica.

'We're staying at the Star Hotel in Adamsville.'

'So are we,' Erica repeated.

'They say its the best hotel for married couples to stay.'

'Oh, we're not married,' said Erica.

The remark brought a frown of disapproval from the woman and a smile from Milton. Erica caught the smile and dug him in the ribs.

Afterwards conversation petered out. Milton contented himself with staring out through the window, while Erica produced a novel from her bag and soon lost herself in it.

The Star Hotel turned out to be a large hotel, which might have been an elegant one in its heyday, but now was definitely in need of several coats of paint and some repairs on its wood-work.

Erica caught Milton studying the hotel.

'I'm sorry that your first visit to a hotel isn't to one of the poshest. This one was recommended to me by one of the ladies in Cotterton.'

'It's all right. Anyhow it's the best hotel for married couples.'

Erica aimed to tap him with her fan, but he adroitly side-stepped.

'If you keep on hitting me, I'll be black and blue by the time we reach Chicago,' he informed her.

In fact the train journey to Chicago was much more pleasant. Although there were several other people in the carriage there was more room than on the stage. This suited Milton since he was able to stretch out his long legs. He again spent most of the journey staring out through the window. However the scenery was much more varied than the flat prairie which had constituted most of the stage journey.

After a couple of hours Erica put away her book.

'I'm going to close my eyes,' she told him. 'I didn't get much sleep in the hotel last night. I can never sleep in a strange bed.'

She was soon asleep. After a while she slipped down in her seat and without opening her eyes she tried to make herself more comfortable. Milton came to her rescue by putting his arm around her. She leaned against him with a sigh of contentment.

They stayed like that for much of the rest of the journey. When she eventually opened her eyes she stared at him without moving. Their faces were close together. The woman opposite observed them interestedly. They were a striking couple. The woman had noticed that Erica was not wearing a wedding ring, so they were obviously a courting couple. While their heads were close together the woman would have sworn that the young lady intended to kiss the man. To her disappointment Erica drew away. Well, maybe she was embarrassed by the fact that they were in a public railway carriage, the woman decided, charitably.

They arrived in Chicago. It was a bustling city with horse-drawn trams.

'Have you been here before?' Milton asked Erica.

'Yes, once. When I was younger. I've got an aunt who lives in the city.'

They caught one of the trams to the hotel. It was named the Great Western. This one was an elegant hotel with a uniformed doorman at the door. They were shown up their rooms on the third floor. Milton waited until Erica had entered her room before going into his. He was impressed by the size of the room. He was even more impressed when he found that the room was equipped with running water.

He stripped to the waist and was having a wash when there was a knock at the door.

'Who is it?' he demanded.

Erica's voice answered. 'It's me.'

Milton found a towel and put it around him before opening the door.

'I see you're using the facilities,' she stated. Her eyes strayed to the stamped mark on his arm.

'I might as well make the most of them.'

'If you ever want a hot bath there are public baths in town where you can have one.'

'I don't think so,' he said, shortly. More so than he had intended.

Why didn't I keep my mouth shut? she told herself irritably. The last thing he would want would be a public bath where the brand on his arm would be visible to all.

'Dinner is in half an hour,' she announced.

'I'll call for you,' he told her.

⋆ ⋆ ⋆

Two days later Erica took Milton to meet her aunt.

'You'll like Aunt Emma,' she told him.

Erica had sent a telegram to her aunt from the hotel and the older woman was expecting her.

Aunt Emma was a petite fifty-year-old. She greeted Erica with a kiss and hugged her as if she was loath to let her go.

'I thought you'd forgotten about your old aunt,' she said at last.

'You're not old,' replied Erica. 'I'd like you to meet my companion, Adam.'

If Aunt Emma thought it was strange that Erica was travelling with a male companion, her face didn't register any surprise.

'Pleased to meet you, Adam,' she said.

'It's my pleasure,' he replied, with a slight bow.

Aunt Emma had arranged an afternoon tea for them.

'When Erica was living in Boston,' she explained to Adam, 'the custom there was to have afternoon tea. So I've had cakes and sandwiches prepared exactly as it was then. I hope you like it.'

'I'm sure I will,' he replied.

After the meal, when Adam was sitting outside in the garden smoking a cigar, Aunt Emma and Erica were in the sitting-room, drinking their coffee.

'Well?' demanded Aunt Emma.

'Well what?' demanded Erica.

'Don't play the innocent with me young lady. Where did you find such a pleasant young man?'

'He isn't exactly what he seems. He used to kill men for a living — he was a bounty hunter. Then he was thrown in jail on a trumped-up charge. He was eventually released, then he came to work for me.'

'Well, whatever he was, he's changed. He seems a perfect gentleman. And you're in love with him.'

'Don't be silly.' Erica blushed.

'Oh, you probably don't realize it now, but you will at some time in the future.'

'You've been reading too many dime novels.'

'I only hope that you realize that you are in love with him before it's too late.'

'Anyhow, how can I love him? I've been brought up as a boy. As you know my father wanted a boy so that's how I was brought up. Now for the past few years I've been running the ranch as a man would have run it. What can I know about love?'

'As I said, I hope you find out before it's too late,' repeated her aunt.

Their stay in Chicago eventually came to an end. While they were waiting to catch the tram to the station, Adam cleared his throat; he appeared slightly embarrassed. Erica glanced at him.

'I just want to say this,' he began. 'I've enjoyed our stay in Chicago. I enjoyed meeting your aunt. And I've enjoyed your company.'

'Thank you for telling me. It's been a lovely holiday.' She kissed him on the cheek.

6

The gunslinger Simms and Lugg were waiting for the stage to come in.

'You won't want me around when you kill Milton, will you?' demanded Lugg, anxiously.

'You can stay in the background. But not too far away. I'll want you as a witness to your father that I've killed him.'

'Where are you going to do it?'

'At the same place where I shot Rand. They won't be expecting an ambush. They'll be tired after their long journey. All they'll want to do will be to get back to their ranch.'

There were several people waiting for the stage although Simms and Lugg hadn't mixed with them. In fact they were on the other side of the road.

'You know what will happen when the stage comes in?' demanded Simms.

'Miss Chambers and Milton will get off it,' suggested Lugg.

'Yes, then what will happen?' A note of irritation had crept into the gun-slinger's tone. Why did he have to be saddled with an idiot like this?

Lugg's brow was creased, showing that he was indulging in a pastime which was foreign to him — thinking.

'Milton will go — where?' prompted Simms.

Lugg's expression brightened.

'To the livery stable.'

'To the livery stable,' Simms repeated, slowly. 'Then while he's at the livery stable what do we do?'

'We wait until he's fetched the buggy, then we follow them.'

'No, you fool.' Simms half-shouted the remark. He instantly looked around to see whether anyone had overheard. But the small group of people were all on the other side of the street. And they were gazing in the direction where the stage would come from.

Lugg turned white with anger.

Although Simms wasn't aware of the fact, the one thing that Lugg hated above all else was to be called a fool. It was an epithet which had been bestowed on him at an early age by his companions in school. At first, because of his size, he had been able to bloody the noses of those who called him a fool. But gradually he had been fighting boys who were just as big as him. The result was he had started losing the fights. The scars caused by the insult, however, were so embedded in his mind that now and then they surfaced. As they did at that moment. Without thinking he hit Simms full in the face with his fist.

Simms staggered with the force of the punch. He would have fallen except that there was a door behind him. He was able to hold on to the handle to try to regain his balance.

The altercation had not passed unnoticed by those waiting on the opposite side of the road. Here was something interesting happening that could help to pass the minutes away before the stage arrived. Simms was trying to stem the blood that was flowing from his nose with a handkerchief.

'Look what you've done,' he hissed. 'You've spoiled everything.'

'You shouldn't have called me a fool,' said Lugg, stubbornly.

'I can't go ahead with the plan now.' Simms was uncomfortably aware of the interested stares of the spectators on the other side of the road.

'You shouldn't have called me a fool,' reiterated Lugg.

'Wait until your father hears about this. It's nothing to what he'll be calling you.'

Lugg slowly digested the thought. From the pained expression on his face it was obvious that he was not looking forward to his meeting with his father.

'Why can't we go ahead with the plan?' he demanded.

The watchers opposite had nearly all turned their attention to scanning the road ahead for the first sign of the stage. The disturbance which had momentarily been of great interest now seemed to have fizzled out, although the smaller guy still looked as though he was having trouble in stopping his nose from bleeding.

'The whole point was that the exercise should be a secret,' hissed Simms. 'Instead of which we've got half the population of Cotterton watching us.'

'Oh, I don't know,' said Lugg, trying to placate him. 'There are only a couple of dozen over the road.'

At that moment there was a cheer from some of the youngsters who were watching for the stage. It had obviously come into sight.

'What are we going to do now?' demanded Lugg.

'We're going to wait here,' growled Simms.

Soon they could all see the stage in the distance. There was a hushed expectancy from the watchers as it approached. The sound of the hoofs of the six horses could be heard beating their tattoo to announce their imminent arrival. Although for the past few miles the horses had been flagging after so many miles, it was as if they sensed that they were coming to the end of their journey. Their manes fluttered in the breeze as they galloped the last few hundred yards to the halt.

'Wo-o-o-oah!' shouted the driver.

There was a bustle of activity as the passengers began to disembark. Lugg and Simms stared at them with varying expressions. Lugg was open-mouthed with a childlike excitement at seeing the arrival of the stage and the passengers leaving it. Simms's gaze just concentrated on two of the passengers. They were easily identified. They were the youngest couple leaving the stage. The man helped the woman down the steps. For a fleeting moment Simms thought about going ahead with his original plan. But he dismissed it as soon as it surfaced. His nose was still bleeding, and he would be in no condition to concentrate on shooting the guy named Milton who had just set off in the direction of the livery stable.

No, Milton would have a stay of execution. Simms smiled grimly at the thought.

7

The atmosphere in Trimble's study was electric. Simms had explained to Trimble how the proposed killing had been postponed because of the argument he had had with Lugg.

'You say Lugg hit you?' Trimble's voice was deceptive, but his fists were clenched threateningly. Lugg wondered whether his father would hit him. True, he hadn't done so for several years. But when he was younger he had been beaten regularly. The implement used was an old leather belt which hung on a hook in the hall. Lugg knew that the belt was still there, even though it hadn't been used for several years.

'How could you be so stupid?' Miles addressed the statement to his brother.

'He riled me,' snapped Lugg. He could argue with his twin brother without any loss of face. They had quarrelled ever since they were a few months old. Often the arguments ended in a fight, which he would invariably win, since he was bigger than Miles.

'Why should I be cursed with a pair of idiot sons?' Trimble's shout was unanswered, since he directed it towards the ceiling.

'I had nothing to do with it, Dad,' protested Miles.

'No, maybe I should have sent you,' conceded his father. 'I doubt whether you would have hit our guest of honour.'

Simms, having delivered his version of the events which had taken place about an hour before was now seated, smoking a thin cigar. His attitude suggested that he had detached himself from the family quarrel which was raging around him.

Trimble clenched and unclenched his fists. Lugg stared at them as though hypnotized. Was this the first step towards having the belt again?

To Lugg's relief his father's next

remark was delivered in a more normal tone.

'All right, all of you get out,' he stated. 'I've got to work out what our next move will be. I should have thought of it before. We're trying to get rid of the wrong person.'

★　★　★

A couple of days later the sheriff of Cotterton rode up to the Big C ranch. The sheriff, a middle-aged portly figure who looked as though if he ever had to physically chase any criminals he would stand little chance of catching them, took his hat off and mopped his brow.

'Sit down, Sheriff,' said Erica, politely.

He sat on the other armchair in the study. It creaked beneath his weight.

'It's Mr Milton I want to see,' he stated.

'If it's private, I'll leave you two alone,' said Erica.

'No, it's nothing personal. It's just that he's wanted in Masonville.'

'Why am I wanted in Masonville?' demanded a puzzled Milton.

'I've just received a telegram from the sheriff there. It's to do with the Smollet gang.'

'Have they caught any more of them?'

'Yes. A few. The sheriff wants you to go to Masonville to testify against them.'

'I don't see that I can be much of a witness for the prosecution. I only met the members of the gang after they were convicted. When we were all chained up together,' he ended, bitterly.

Erica shot him a sympathetic glance.

'So why does the sheriff want Adam?' she enquired.

'It's a matter of identification,' stated the sheriff. 'A few of them are denying they were ever members of the gang.'

'A couple of them are dead,' supplied Milton. 'I killed them when I was a bounty hunter.'

'So you were a bounty hunter?' The sheriff wiped his perspiring forehead with a large handkerchief.

'That's how I became falsely accused of being a member of the gang. They wanted to get their own back. Especially Smollet.'

'Adam was a bounty hunter but now he has a responsible job working for me,' said Erica, coldly.

'If you could see your way clear to allow Milton to go to Masonville. It would help to put some criminals behind bars where they belong.'

'It's up to Adam.' Erica glanced at him enquiringly.

'Well, if it will put then behind bars for the next ten years I'll be happy to help.'

The sheriff glanced at Erica for confirmation.

'As I said, it's Adam's decision.'

'Right. I'll telegraph the sheriff to say that he'll be on his way.'

The sheriff stood up.

When he had left Milton waited for Erica to dismiss him. Instead she sat at her desk and pushed her fingers through her short hair with a gesture that was familiar to him.

'I don't trust him,' she announced.

'Because he failed to find the killer of your previous manager?'

'I suppose so. I believe he's in the pay of Trimble,' she said, bitterly. 'He should be concentrating on putting him behind bars instead of dragging you to Masonville to testify against some outlaws.'

'I'll be all right. I'll be back tomorrow — once I've made my statement. Anyhow you said there's not much work for me to do around here at the moment.'

'No, I suppose not,' she said with a sigh. 'You'll take care, won't you?'

An hour later he set off. He had assumed that Erica was still in her study. However she was watching from her bedroom.

Why was she feeling so downhearted at seeing him leave? He would be returning tomorrow. Then her right-hand man would be back and everything would be the same as it had been.

But were things the same? Things had changed since they had come back from Chicago and it was difficult to know why. She knew that the blame rested entirely with her. When they were in Chicago everything had been perfect. She and Adam had become firm friends. Yes, those were the words: 'firm friends'. He had been an excellent companion. He had known when to keep quiet — she liked the long periods of silence they had shared together. He had also known when to join in the conversation — particularly when they had visited Aunt Emma. He had entertained them with some of the tales about the nuns who had brought him up. They had both been surprised to hear that the nuns often spent some of their time telling each other rude jokes. He had made them chuckle at some of the less rude ones which he had overheard when the boys used to eavesdrop on the nuns.

Another pleasant surprise she had received was while they were staying at the hotel. There had been a dinner-dance. They were watching the dancers and she had assumed that Adam couldn't dance. To her surprise he had asked her to have a waltz. He had danced it perfectly. He had told her that the nuns had taught them how to dance.

Why couldn't things be just as perfect now as they had been then? She brushed away a tear as she watched Adam disappear into the distance.

8

Erica would have been even more disturbed if she had seen in which direction the sheriff rode after leaving her ranch. Instead of heading for Cotterton he had headed straight for the Trimble spread.

He arrived at the ranch about half an hour later. Calan and Mars were keeping guard at the gate. They had found that their jobs had hardly varied from when they were guarding Erica's ranch. The only difference was that Trimble employed fewer cowboys than Erica and so there were fewer to share the bunkhouse with. The only blot on the horizon, in fact, to their having a nice easy existence was named Lugg. They had soon found out that he was a bully. As such he took delight in trying to rile them. This would inevitably have led to a fight. In which case it would have been just as inevitable that Lugg would have won.

This particular morning they were surprised to see the sheriff approaching. They had both been around Erica's ranch long enough to know that the sheriff was noted for his idleness. If he could possibly do so he would stay seated in his office for days on end. If there were any errands to attend to he would dispatch his deputy.

The two watched his approach with a certain measure of puzzlement.

'I wonder what he wants?' whispered Calan.

'He wants to see old man Trimble,' replied Mars.

Sure enough the sheriff drew up close to them. He motioned to one of them to hold his horse while he dismounted.

Trimble was alone in his study when Mars ushered the sheriff in.

'Sit down, Sheriff,' said Trimble, affably. To Mars he said: 'I don't want to be disturbed under any circumstances. Do you understand?'

'Certainly, sir,' replied Mars, as he beat a hasty retreat.

The sheriff's reception was warmer than the one he had received in Erica's study. Trimble offered him a glass of whiskey, which he eagerly accepted.

'I've just been to see Miss Chambers,' he stated. 'She didn't even offer me a glass of water.' He hurriedly downed his whiskey. It was a signal for Trimble to offer him another. He duly obliged.

'Now, let's get down to business,' said Trimble. 'You say you've been to see Miss Chambers?'

'That's right. I've arranged for Milton to be out of sight for a couple of days. I told them a cock-and-bull story that he is wanted by the sheriff in Masonville.'

'That sounds promising,' said Trimble, as he sipped his whiskey.

'So it means you can go ahead with your plan.'

'That's right.'

'As I told you before, I don't want to know what that plan is. I've just carried out my part in getting rid of Milton. The other thing is, I want you to carry out your part of the agreement.'

Trimble nodded. 'I've got two thousand dollars in the bureau which you will take with you when you go away. The rest of the agreement will come into force when our two ranches are joined together. You will receive enough money to let you retire in comfort with a handsome pension.'

For the first time since entering the study the sheriff looked doubtful.

'This doesn't mean you're going to harm Miss Chambers, does it?'

'Certainly not,' asserted Trimble, positively. 'I just wanted a day where I could spend some time with Miss Chambers. If I can be alone with her it will give me a chance to explain the advantages of joining our two ranches together.'

'Yes, that makes sense,' said the

sheriff, with a large degree of relief in his voice.

He left shortly afterwards, having refused the offer of another glass of whiskey.

Mars and Calan, having watched him disappear with a certain relief, were surprised when they were summoned in to Trimble's study.

'I want you two to come with me,' he stated.

'Where to?' demanded Mars.

'We're going to pay a visit to Miss Chambers.'

'We're not exactly her favourite workers,' said Calan. 'Especially after that swine Milton took over.'

'Well, Milton is out of the way. That's why we're going to pay your ex-boss a visit.'

'It will certainly make things easier if Milton is out of the way,' stated Mars.

'Those are my sentiments exactly,' said Trimble.

9

Erica was surprised to see Trimble, Calan and Mars riding up to the house. If Trimble had been on his own she would have given the order to one of her cowboys not to let him in. But since he was accompanied by two men whom she knew — although she didn't trust them, the situation had changed. She reluctantly agreed to see them when her housekeeper announced their arrival.

'To what do I owe this honour?' she asked, coldly, when they entered her study.

'We've come on a peace mission,' Trimble announced, pleasantly.

'If you expect a pipe of peace here, you've come to the wrong place,' snapped Erica.

'I wonder if I can ask you a favour?' enquired Trimble.

'What is it?'

'My old bones aren't what they used to be. Do you mind if I sit down while we discuss business?'

'I've got nothing to discuss with you. But you can sit down anyway.' She waved him to the vacant armchair.

'The matter I've come to discuss is private, so we won't need these.' He indicated Calan and Mars.

'They can go and water their horses while we're discussing whatever you've come for.'

'Thanks,' said Calan.

Trimble waited until they had disappeared through the door, then he spoke.

'I've come to make you an increased offer for your ranch,' he said.

'Then you're wasting your time. It's not for sale. As you well know.'

'Well, you might as well hear my offer. It's double the offer I made two years ago. It's ten thousand dollars for the ranch, plus five dollars a head for every one of your cattle.'

Erica was on the point of flatly

refusing the offer when she paused.

'It's a good bargain,' Trimble pursued, seeing her hesitation. 'It's more than I offered you previously.'

Erica crossed to the window and stared out at the range.

'How many head of cattle do you have?' he asked.

'About two thousand.'

'So that's ten thousand for the cattle and ten thousand for the ranch. Twenty thousand in all. Think what you can do with twenty thousand.'

In spite of the fact that she didn't trust Trimble any further than she could see him, the offer was tempting. She wouldn't have to rule the ranch from day to day with an iron fist. She would be able to relax. She would, of course, go back to Boston. She had spent long enough in this dusty, dirty part of the world. She had spent enough time giving orders and generally behaving like a man. She had spent enough time dressed like a man. How she longed to put on women's clothes — petticoats and a frock in the morning.

'Pour yourself a drink,' she said, without turning round. Trimble obliged, with a smile of satisfaction on his face. He knew he had Miss Chambers where he wanted her.

Erica was thinking about the few days she and Milton had spent in Chicago. It was civilized living — far removed from this humdrum existence. She had gone to the opera one evening. She had asked Milton if he wanted to accompany her, but he had politely refused, saying that he would prefer to go to watch the fights at the boxing-booth. So she had gone to see *La Traviata* by Verdi. She had unashamedly wept at Violeta's death. Here on the ranch she had always kept her emotions under tight control, but to be able to weep was an untold relief.

'It's a good offer,' Trimble repeated.

Yes, there was no doubt about it. It was a good offer. She would be able to go back to Boston, buy a nice house and live comfortably on the interest for the rest of her life. She had only taken over the ranch because her father had died and she wished to prove that she was quite capable of running the ranch. Well, she'd proved it. She'd been here now for four years. She'd served her apprenticeship. It was time to live her life as she wished to live it. Not at the dictates of her dead father.

'I'll want the transfer documents drawn up by my own lawyer.'

'No problem,' said Trimble, pouring himself another whiskey.

'Ten thousand dollars for the ranch and five dollars a head for all my cattle.'

'That's right.'

'I'll want extra for my prize Hereford bull.'

'We can arrange that when your lawyer draws up the transfer. By the way, where does he live?'

'In Chicago.'

'It'll take him a few days to get here.'

'Two days if I telegraph him right away.'

'Right. You do that. I'll have to arrange with my bank in Adamsville to transfer the money. May I ask where you intend living when you leave the ranch?'

'Boston,' she replied, with more than a hint of relief in her voice.

10

Lugg had cornered Simms in the sitting-room of the Trimble ranch. Simms was cleaning his revolvers.

'Get away from me,' said Simms, leaving no doubt in Lugg's slow mind that he was an unwelcome intruder.

'I've got something important to tell you,' Lugg ventured.

'Like you have found out that two and two make four?' sneered Simms.

Lugg controlled his temper with an effort. It was a couple of days since he had bloodied Simms' nose. He would do it again if the gunslinger pushed him too far. Of course the sight of the twin revolvers on the table and the slick way Simms was handling them was an additional factor which he would have to take into account this time and which would probably prevent him from taking any physical action.

'I've come here with the friendliest of intentions,' Lugg protested.

'Just say what you've got to say and leave me alone,' snapped Simms.

'You know when Pa said that you would be getting rid of the wrong person when you killed Milton?'

'Yes?' Simms looked up from polishing a gun.

'Well, he meant Miss Chambers.'

'I know that. So what?'

'Well, the sheriff has just been here.'

'I know. I saw him. I keep out of the way of sheriffs.'

Lugg didn't appreciate the grim humour of the comment.

'I overheard them talking.'

'You listen at keyholes, do you?'

Lugg ignored the snide remark.

'The sheriff said that he had arranged for Milton to leave the Chambers's ranch. He had pretended that the guy was wanted by the sheriff of Masonville.'

For the first time Simms showed some interest in the conversation.

'Go on.'

'I didn't hear much more of the conversation because Pa called Mars and Calan into the study and I had to make myself scarce.'

'So Milton is out of the way,' said Simms, thoughtfully.

'That's right. Oh, I did hear that Pa had paid the sheriff two thousand dollars for getting rid of Milton.'

'So it looks as though the action is about to start.' Simms picked up one of the revolvers and squinted down the barrel.

'That's right,' said Lugg, excitedly. 'So there's nothing stopping you going ahead and killing Miss Chambers.'

'Right. I'll see your father and get permission from him.'

'He isn't on the ranch,' said Lugg. 'He's gone off somewhere with Mars and Calan. I guess they've gone into Cotterton.'

'That was a stupid thing to do when there was unfinished business to attend to,' said Simms, irritably.

'It doesn't make any difference though, does it?'

'How do you mean?'

'Well, Pa's going to pay you for killing Miss Chambers. It doesn't matter whether he's here to see you off.'

'I'd rather get it over with.' Simms holstered one of the guns.

'Well, I'll tell Pa that I gave you permission to kill her. After all I'm the next in charge. I'm the eldest of the twins.'

Simms felt that it was a big temptation. They had all heard Trimble say that he would be getting rid of the wrong person if he killed Milton. That could only mean that Miss Chambers was the intended victim. That, of course, made sense, since with Miss Chambers out of the way Trimble would have a free hand to take over her ranch.

There was another matter, too, which had a bearing on whether to go ahead and kill her now, without waiting for

Trimble's permission. He was bored with the inactivity. He was bored with hanging about the ranch. He had been here now for well over a fortnight. True, he had managed to kill the manager of the Chambers ranch. And he had been well paid for it. But now the time had come to move on. The money he had had and the money he would have would mean that he could live like a king for several months — at least until his next assignment.

Lugg waited with uncharacteristic sensitivity while Simms made up his mind.

'How long ago was it when your father went into Cotterton?'

'About half an hour ago. When he goes to Cotterton he usually stays there for a few hours.'

'I don't want to hang around here any longer.' It was obvious that Simms had come to a decision by the way he deliberately put his other gun in the holster.

'Then you'll go and kill her now?'

Lugg's voice was full of excitement.

'That's what I'm getting paid for.' Simms stood up.

'I'll get your horse,' said Lugg, eagerly.

11

It was late in the afternoon when Milton rode into Masonville. He had covered the eleven miles between Cotterton and Masonville at a leisurely pace. Truth to tell he had been glad to get away from the ranch for a few hours. He would call to see the sheriff. Probably the lawman would want him to make a written statement. When he had completed it he would find a saloon. He would have a few beers and a meal. He would book a bed for the night, then tomorrow he would set off back to Miss Chambers's ranch.

It was strange that he was now thinking of her as Miss Chambers. Not as Erica, a name which he had used for several days. What had happened to the relationship which he had enjoyed when they had been in Chicago? There was no doubt that she had seemed an entirely different person when they had been there. There was no doubt too, that she had let her hair down — figuratively of course. It was as if, when they had returned to the ranch, that she didn't want to get too close to him. It was as if she regretted sharing those moments of happy relaxation with him.

Well, she need not concern herself on his part. Chicago was now almost a forgotten memory. He had put it in the back of his mind. It had been a few happy days — nothing more. The stay in Chicago was something which he hadn't expected and which he had accepted gratefully. But it was over. If Miss Chambers wanted them to revert to their previous boss — employee relationship, then it was all right by him.

He passed the sheriff's office on his way down Main Street. He stopped at the livery stable.

'Will you feed and water my horse?' he asked the wizened old man who was in charge.

'When will you be collecting him?'

'Tomorrow morning.'

'That will be a dollar.'

Milton tossed the old man the coin. Five minutes later he entered the sheriff's office.

The sheriff, who was seated behind his desk, was a slim, dark-haired young man who looked too young to be a sheriff. He glanced up from going through some papers.

'What can I do for you?' he asked, pleasantly.

'It's what I can do for you,' replied Milton.

'I don't understand.'

'You sent a telegram to the sheriff of Cotterton. The telegram said that you wanted to see me. My name is Milton.'

'There must be some mistake. I never sent such a telegram.'

'But he said he'd received it yesterday. It's about the Smollet gang.'

'I never sent a telegram to the sheriff of Cotterton and I don't know anything about the Smollet gang.' The sheriff was beginning to get annoyed.

'But why should he tell me that you had sent a telegram?' There was puzzlement and anger in his voice.

'I've got no idea. Who are the Smollet gang anyhow?'

'They're a gang of outlaws. I managed to put some of them behind bars. I also killed a couple of them. I was a bounty hunter.'

'So you killed a few outlaws?' There was a new respect in the sheriff's voice.

'Yes.' Milton was studying the drawings of the outlaws on the board. 'Here are some of the Smollet gang.' He pointed to a few of the drawings.

'Hey! That's interesting. Are you sure?'

'I should be. I was chained up with some of them for a couple of years. I was wrongly accused of being one of the members of the gang.'

'If you can show me which are the members of the gang it might help to bring them back to justice.'

Milton pointed them out to the sheriff who added the words Smollet gang under the drawings.

'So they all must have escaped otherwise they wouldn't be on this board,' said Milton, thoughtfully.

'That's right. They were being transferred by train to the state prison. They managed to overpower a guard. Then they jumped off the train. They have never been recaptured. Well, thanks for the information about them.'

'That's all right.'

'Can I get you a cup of coffee? I'm making one for myself.'

'That would be great.'

While the sheriff was making the coffee a question was churning round in Milton's head. Why had the sheriff of Cotterton sent him here on a wild-goose chase? Was it an honest mistake or was there something sinister behind it? The more he thought about it the more he concluded that there must be some ulterior motive for the sheriff's action. In the first place it was extremely unusual for the sheriff to deliver the message himself. It was common knowledge that he hardly moved from his office. If he had any messages to deliver he would send his deputy. So why hadn't he on this occasion?

Suppose he had been sent on this trumped-up errand in order to get him out of the way. His blood ran cold at the thought. There was a strong suspicion that the sheriff had somehow been involved in the killing of the previous manager of Erica's ranch. It had been obvious when he arrived at the ranch that Erica disliked him. She had pointedly not offered to give him any refreshments. So what if her suspicions were true? What if the sheriff had colluded with Trimble in order to get him out of the way so that Erica could be the next on the hit list? It all fitted. The way would be open for the gunslinger, whoever he was, to ride up to the ranch and shoot Erica.

Oh, God, no! Let his assumptions be wrong.

The sheriff returned with the coffees.

'Here you are.' He looked around for Milton, but there was no sign of him. Well, that's ingratitude for you. Having gone to the trouble of making him a cup of coffee he's gone without even saying good-bye.

12

Simms had started out for the Chambers' ranch about two hours before Milton arrived in Masonville. He had resolved to get the killing over as soon as possible. Lugg, while not the most reliable of associates, had opened the way for the deed by stating that the sheriff had arranged for Milton to go to Masonville. With Milton out of the way the coast was clear. He would have preferred to have had the killing sanctioned by Trimble before he carried it out. But it was only a small matter of dotting the i's and crossing the t's. He had been in Trimble's study when he had stated that he intended getting rid of Miss Chambers and not Milton, as he and the others had expected.

So he had to kill a woman. Well, it was of no great matter whether he killed a man or a woman. He had received $1,000 for the last killing. And he would receive $1,000 for this one. On the other hand, maybe killing a woman should come dearer. Perhaps he should have asked for an extra $5,000. He smiled grimly at the thought.

He knew the terrain over which he was riding. He had spent over two weeks at the Trimble ranch and for some of that time, in order to relieve the monotony, he had ridden on the range. The fact that the two ranches were not fenced in made it easy for him to ride for an hour or so without seeing any other riders — except at a distance. It also meant that he had discovered how he could arrive at Miss Chambers' ranch without taking the obvious route. It would mean an extra half an hour to be added to the time he would arrive there, but he was in no hurry. Milton would be away for the whole day, which meant that time was on his side.

As he rode leisurely along he mused about what he would do with the $2,000. Where would he go to? There were several attractive possibilities. Of course, San Francisco was the obvious choice — Sin City as it was now known. Yes, he'd like to savour some of its sins. The only problem was he would have to travel by train to get there. This was in fact a major problem. He had found that whenever he travelled on a train he was invariably sick. It was an affliction which was both stressful and annoying. He knew that young children were often affected this way. But for a man of thirty years to be so afflicted was no joke.

So if San Francisco was out, what alternatives were there? Of course he could go round the several towns which had mushroomed up during the past ten years, after the wars with the Indians had been more or less settled. Yes, he could do that. But somehow that didn't appeal to him. He had called in at most of them during his travels over the years and one town was very much like another. No, what he wanted was somewhere different. Suddenly the idea sprang to his mind — Mexico.

Yes! He became excited at the thought. He had always wanted to go to Mexico. Now he would have the opportunity and, more important, the money. Of course it would probably take a couple of weeks for him to ride there. But there would be no hurry. At least he wouldn't have to travel by train. He smiled at the thought.

The Chambers' ranch came into view. He had only seen a couple of cowboys in the distance, but now here was the moment of truth. Could he ride up to the ranch without being observed?

There was a stand of trees at a convenient distance from the house. He approached them slowly. He was facing the side of house and he had no idea in which room he would find Miss Chambers.

He reached the trees. His first objective was secured. He felt like a soldier who had to carry out one task after another. His next was to approach the house and try to reach the stone wall which ran around the house. He unsheathed his rifle. He glanced around. Again there was nobody in sight. Now for his second objective. He took a deep breath and sprinted the couple of hundred yards towards the wall.

He reached it gasping for breath. He hadn't realized how much he was suffering from lack of fitness. He even found himself trembling slightly with the sudden exertion. This wasn't a good omen. It was essential that there should be no tremor in his hand before he pulled the trigger. He had always prided himself on his steadiness of nerve. Indeed it was a vital ingredient in his line of business. Now he found that after his exertions his hands were trembling. He held them out in front to test for any involuntary movement. Yes, there was no doubt about it. There was a slight tremor.

Well, he'd just have to wait a few minutes until his hands returned to normal. While he was waiting he scanned the house. It was about fifty yards away. This time there would be no difficulty if he had to run the intervening distance. There was a convenient side door which he assumed could lead to the kitchen. He was idly glancing at the bedrooms when he received an incredible surprise. Miss Chambers was standing in one of the bedroom windows. She was perfectly framed in the window as she stared out across the prairie.

He didn't hesitate. He would never have another chance like this. He had already loaded his rifle. He rested it carefully on the wall and took aim. He took a deep breath the way he always did when he was using a rifle.

He squeezed the trigger. The sound of the report startled some crows which had settled in a nearby tree. He was aware of the 'crack' of the glass as the window splintered. The other sound was his grunt of satisfaction as the red stain on Miss Chambers' white shirt testified that his shot had been successful.

13

Milton was riding like the wind towards Cotterton. His horse's hoofs seemed to be beating a repetitive question: Would he be in time?

What a fool he had been not to have seen it coming. There had been enough clues for a half-wit to have spotted them. But he had blithely ignored them. Erica had said that she didn't trust the sheriff. He had ignored the statement, partly because he had been glad to get away from the ranch for a couple of days.

To think that he had ignored her suspicions about the sheriff because he was peeved about the way she had treated him after they had returned from Chicago. When he examined his reaction in the cold light of day it seemed unbelievable. That he, a thirty-year-old man, could be so childish. He had behaved like one of the jilted lovers some of the nuns used to read avidly about in the dime magazines.

What would he find when he arrived at the ranch? He tried to blot the thought out of his mind. He kept spurring his horse to greater effort. But he realized that it was only so fast that he could force the animal to gallop. He only knew that the eleven miles between Masonville and Cotterton were seeming like an eternity. He calculated that he had at least four to go. The horse was tiring already. Should he slow the animal down or hope that it would have enough stamina to last the distance. He chose the latter and gave it another kick with his heels.

He had been hired as a bodyguard. Some bodyguard! At the slightest excuse he left the person he was guarding in the lurch. He didn't deserve to be guarding a henhouse let alone a lovely lady. He swore that if the gunman had harmed her he would hunt him down. Even if it took him the rest of his life.

Half an hour later he rode up to the ranch. The first thing he noticed was a white horse tied to the front rails. His heart lurched when he recognized it as the doctor's horse. The doctor had come to the ranch a couple of days before to attend to one of the cowboys and there was no mistaking his horse.

Milton sprang from his horse. He rushed into the house. There was the sound of sobbing coming from Erica's bedroom. Milton raced up the stairs and pushed open the bedroom door.

Erica was lying in bed. She was unconscious and judging from her pallor she could have departed from this life.

'Is she — dead?' he asked.

'I'd say that at the moment she's hanging on to life by the thinnest of threads,' said the doctor.

Erica's Mexican maid was crouched in the corner sobbing.

'When did it happen? Who did it?' demanded Milton.

'How do you know she was shot?' asked the doctor, keenly.

'It's a long story. But I know.'

'She was standing by the window.' The doctor pointed to the broken glass. 'Someone shot her from behind that wall.'

'I sent for the sheriff,' the maid announced, between sobs.

Milton studied Erica. She seemed to be barely breathing.

'Will she live?'

'It's up to God now. I've done all I can. The bullet is still lodged inside her.'

'I can't do anything here. But there is somewhere where I can do something.'

The doctor glanced at Milton, surprised at the raw anger in his voice.

'You think you know who shot her?'

'I'm positive I know who's behind it.'

He leaned over Erica until his face was close to hers.

'I'm sorry I wasn't here. But I promise you one thing. I'll get the bastard who did this, if it takes me the rest of my life.'

Was he wrong, or was there the slightest flicker of movement from her eyes, as if she was telling him that she had understood his message?

'Hadn't you better wait for the sheriff?' asked the doctor as Milton headed for the door.

'That skunk? If he came here there'll probably be another shooting,' replied Milton.

14

Trimble was in his study screaming like a demented dervish. Lugg was cowering in the corner. Simms was looking on interestedly.

'You've what?' yelled Trimble.

'I told Simms here to go ahead and kill Miss Chambers. You weren't here so I told him.'

'You told him?' No stage actor could have poured more scorn into the statement. 'You numskull. You idiot. You half-wit.' Trimble ran out of insults but it was only because he had run out of breath.

'But you said you wanted her killed, Pa,' whined Lugg.

'I never said I wanted her killed,' Trimble emphasized every word as he spoke through clenched teeth.

'But you said you wanted to get rid of her.' Simms spoke for the first time after announcing that the killing had been successful.

'You keep out of this. You've done enough damage as it is,' snapped Trimble.

Simms's eyes narrowed in what a close acquaintance would recognize as a danger signal. Nobody spoke disparagingly to Simms without him storing it in mind and resolving to avenge himself on the originator of the remark, even if it took months to do so.

'He's quite right, Pa.' Lugg eagerly seized on Simms's support, on the assumption that any support was better than none.

'I didn't want her killed.' Trimble clenched his fists and appealed to heaven.

'But you said — '

'I'd never agree to killing a woman,' he screamed. 'Surely you'd know that.'

'But you did say you wanted to get rid of her.' Simms intervened once more hoping to clear the air.

'Of course I did, you fool. I wanted

to get rid of her so that I could own her ranch. I wanted to buy her out.'

Lugg and Simms digested the statement in silence. Lugg wrestled with its implications. 'But you've tried to buy her out before, and you haven't succeeded,' he said at last.

'I know that,' snapped Trimble. 'So I did the obvious thing. I upped my price.'

'And she accepted?' demanded Lugg.

'Of course she did. I made her an offer she couldn't refuse. I assumed that when I die at least all my money will be invested in cattle. I'll change my will so that you and the other half-wit member of the family won't be able to sell the stock. That way you won't be able to gamble away my money when I've gone.'

'When did you go over to see Miss Chambers?' asked Simms.

'This morning — after the sheriff had called here.'

'You told me he had gone into Cotterton,' said Simms, accusingly.

'How was I to know where he had gone?' Lugg whined. 'I just assumed, that's all.'

'This brainless idiot told you that I had gone into Cotterton. So you rode out to Miss Chambers's ranch. After I had come away from the ranch you rode up to it. And you shot her.'

'Yes, I guess that's how it was,' said Simms, casually.

'What are we going to do now, Pa?' demanded Lugg.

'There's nothing we can do. The sheriff's on our side so he'll conceal the truth. You weren't seen, were you?' He addressed the remark to Simms.

'Of course I wasn't,' the gunslinger answered, scornfully.

'In that case I think you'd better make yourself scarce before the sheriff arrives on the scene.'

'What about my payment?'

'I've paid you for killing Rand. I don't pay gunslingers for killing a woman.'

This time there was no mistaking the

hardening of the expression on Simms's face.

'It wasn't my fault that this idiot gave me a bum steer. I carried out my end of the bargain.'

'And I'm telling you again that I don't pay anyone for killing a woman.'

As Trimble uttered the remark he surreptitiously slid the drawer of his desk open. There was a revolver inside which he intended to seize and reinforce his statement. Simms, who lived by his keen eyes and quick reflexes instantly spotted his intentions. In one lightning movement he drew his gun and shot Trimble in the head.

Lugg's reaction at seeing his father killed was an involuntary one. With a cry like a wounded animal he flung himself at the gunslinger. However he was several yards away and he never reached his objective. Simms shot him when he was in mid-air.

Simms's instant reflexes again came to his aid when he heard a stifled gasp from outside the door. He flung it open. It was obvious that Miles had been eavesdropping and was now haring down the corridor as fast as his legs could carry him.

It wasn't fast enough, since the gunslinger shot him in the back. Simms's next move was to go back into the study and open Trimble's desk. He found what he was looking for in the third drawer — a bundle of dollar bills. He hastily stuffed them in his jacket. He didn't even bother to glance at the bodies as he left the house by the side door.

15

Milton rode up to the Trimble ranch in a cloud of dust. Calan was waiting at the gate. From his expression Milton guessed that there was something amiss.

He jumped off his horse. 'I want to see Trimble,' he snapped.

'You can see him, but it won't do any good.'

'What do you mean?'

'He's been shot. Mars has gone for the sheriff.'

'Trimble — dead?'

'Yes, and the twins — Lugg and Miles.'

'What the hell's going on?'

'The gunslinger killed them. He calls himself Simms.'

'He was the one who shot Erica,' said Milton, as realization dawned.

'Miss Chambers is dead?' Calan's

worried expression changed to genuine concern.

'No. The doctor is with her. He said she's just hanging on to life.'

'That bastard Simms. I never did trust him,' said Calan, venomously.

'Where are the bodies?' demanded Milton.

Calan led him into the house. Miles's body was still in the passage where Simms had shot him. Milton gave him a cursory glance to confirm that he was dead.

'Old man Trimble and Lugg are in the study,' Calan informed him.

Trimble was wedged behind the desk, having slid from his chair. Lugg was still in the corner where he had fallen having tried unsuccessfully to reach Simms.

Milton checked the two bodies.

'When Mars comes back you two get over to Miss Chambers's ranch,' he said. 'If she recovers she will need all the help she can get.'

'Right. I'll be glad to get away from this place.'

Milton was studying the half-open drawers of the desk.

'It looks as though someone has been searching for something in these.'

'Probably Simms. They say that old man Trimble used to keep a lot of money in them.'

'So Simms probably found what he was looking for,' said Milton, thoughtfully.

'More than likely.'

'There's nothing we can do here,' said Milton, as he led the way out of the study. When they were outside he asked: 'How long is it since Mars left to fetch the sheriff?'

'About two hours.'

'Two hours,' said Milton, incredulously. 'He should have been here ages ago.'

Calan shrugged. 'What I've seen of him it probably would have taken him half an hour to get on his horse.'

'So Simms must have got a good couple of hours' start in which ever direction he was going.'

'It didn't take a genius to work that out,' said Calan, sarcastically.

'What kind of horse was Simms riding?' demanded Milton.

Calan thought for a moment. 'A black stallion,' he said, eventually.

'What about the cowboys who were out on the range? How many of them have come back in?'

'Most of them are in the bunkhouse. Once they knew that their boss has been shot, they rode back in.'

'Right. Take me in the bunkhouse.'

Calan led the way. In the bunkhouse about a couple of dozen cowboys had gathered. Most of them were all deep in conversation. They glanced up when the two entered.

'This is Milton,' stated Calan. 'He works for Miss Chambers. He wants to have a word with you.'

'The guy who killed Mr Trimble and his two sons has almost killed Miss Chambers,' Milton announced.

There was a murmur of disbelief from the assembled cowboys. One of them summed up their feeling.

'Get the bastard,' he shouted.

'We might stand a slight chance,' said Milton. 'He's got two hours' lead on us. If we set off in the next half-hour or so there's a faint chance we might catch him.'

'I'm with you,' said one.

'And me. And me.' There was a chorus of agreement.

'Right. Grab some food and bring your blankets. We'll try to catch the murdering gunslinger.'

'When we get him we'll hang him,' said a voice. He had vociferous backing from his comrades.

The cowboys fed and watered their horses while they grabbed some chow for themselves. The housekeeper supplied Milton with some fresh bread and cheese.

'I hope you'll get him,' she said, with feeling. 'I've worked for ten years for Mr Trimble, and I always found him a fair man. That's more than I could say for his wastrel sons,' she added bitterly.

The cowboys had started to gather outside the ranch house. There was a strong measure of excitement in the air. They had unhesitatingly accepted Milton as their leader.

'Which way do we go?' asked one.

'Who saw Simms on his black stallion riding away from the ranch?' demanded Milton.

'I did,' piped up one of the cowboys.

'Which way was he riding?'

'South,' came the unhesitating reply.

'Then that's the way we're heading,' stated Milton.

Some of the cowboys shouted 'Hurrah!' Some waved their hats. Milton couldn't resist a smile at their enthusiasm.

'Right, let's go,' he yelled.

At the command a couple of dozen cowboys set off with high hopes. Milton knew that their only hope of catching Simms lay in the fact that the gunslinger wouldn't be expecting a posse to follow him. After the first hour or so of riding he might slow down.

This could allow the posse to close the gap between them and the gunslinger.

Another possibility, of course, would be that Simms's horse could develop something which could slow him down — a faulty shoe, for example. Anyhow, the cowboys were happy that they were doing something positive to avenge their murdered boss. The main thing was to cover as many miles as they could before nightfall. Then to see what tomorrow would bring.

16

The sheriff rode up to the Trimble ranch about half an hour after the posse had left. He was accompanied by Mars.

'You took your time,' snapped Calan.

'He said he had to wait for his deputy to return,' stated Mars.

'Never mind about that,' said the sheriff, as he dismounted from his horse with the aid of the hitching rail. 'Where are the bodies?'

Calan led him inside. The sheriff's examination of each corpse was perfunctory. The only emotion he displayed was a tightening of the lips when he came to Trimble. If the two watchers attributed the movement to a sense of loss that one of his friends had been murdered, they would have been wrong. In fact he was thinking about the thousands of dollars which he would have received, but which had now indubitably disappeared.

'You say a gunslinger named Simms killed them?' he addressed the remark to Mars.

'That's right.'

'And he rode off?'

'About three hours ago,' supplied Calan. 'If you had hurried here you could have formed the posse yourself.'

'What are you talking about? What posse?' snapped the sheriff.

'That guy Milton formed a posse. They've gone after Simms.'

The fact that they were in the study which was now in semi-darkness probably saved the sheriff. He had paled at the mention that Simms was being chased by a posse. If either of the cowboys had noticed his reaction they could well have put two and two together, and come up with an interesting question. Such as what connection was there between the sheriff and Simms?

'He had no right to form a posse,' blustered the sheriff.

'The men were all behind him. They couldn't wait for you,' snapped Calan.

Three hours' start. They wouldn't stand a chance of catching him. The sheriff began to breathe more easily.

'You've got to go over to Miss Chambers' ranch. She's been shot, too,' Calan announced. 'We're coming with you,' he added.

'Are we?' asked a puzzled Mars.

'Milton said we should go back to the ranch and give any help that might be needed.'

'Oh, I see,' supplied Mars.

'It's Milton this, Milton that,' said the sheriff, the bile having risen in his throat.

'He's only doing your job for you,' stated Calan, rubbing salt in the wound.

They rode over to the Chambers ranch in silence. They were met at the door by the housekeeper.

'The doctor has gone. He said there's nothing more he can do here,' she addressed the remark to Calan and Mars.

'I suppose I'd better go up and see her,' said the sheriff.

They all trooped up the stairs. In the bedroom the sheriff approached the still body with circumspection.

'She hardly seems to be breathing,' he told the housekeeper.

'The doctor said she's hanging on to life by a thread,' she replied.

Back downstairs in the kitchen she offered the three men cups of coffee. While they were drinking it the sheriff spoke.

'I don't suppose anyone saw the killer?' he asked.

'No. The doctor said he must have hidden behind the wall to fire at Miss Chambers.'

'Did the doctor say what sort of gun was used? Was it a rifle or a revolver?'

'If you were going to kill somebody by shooting them from behind the wall, you wouldn't use a revolver,' said Calan, scornfully. 'It wouldn't be accurate enough.'

The sheriff shot him a baleful glare.

'I've got to be sure,' he snapped.

'The doctor said the killer used a rifle. The bullet is still inside her.'

'The poor lamb,' said Mars. Calan's worried face echoed his friend's sentiments. Only the sheriff seemed unmoved by the announcement.

The sheriff finished his coffee.

'I'll have a look at the spot where the killer fired the shot from,' he stated. 'Although I don't expect I will find anything.'

The other watched him leave. Nobody offered to go to the door with him.

'He's a pig of a man,' said the housekeeper.

'We're to stay here while Miss Chambers is ill,' said Calan. 'Milton told us to stay.'

'He's a good man,' she pronounced.

17

The posse had spent a night in a sheltered spot on the edge of a small wood. The following morning they found enough timber to light a fire and were soon devouring the beans supplied by the housekeeper.

Milton was approached by one of the men.

'What chance do you think we have of catching him?'

'It all depends how long he stops in Adamsville. He'll probably stop there to feed his horse. So we'll head for the livery stable. With luck we might find that he has decided to stop for a few hours, and we might catch him.'

'There are two livery stables in Adamsville,' said another cowboy, who had overheard the conversation.

'In that case we'll split up into two parties,' said Milton.

The cowboy passed the information on the others and they soon set off again.

Milton knew that it was important for them to have a target to aim at in order to stop their interest from flagging. Since they were concentrating on arriving at Adamsville, that would hold their interest for the rest of the morning.

In fact it was early in the afternoon when they arrived. Milton called a halt when they reached the outskirts of the town.

'This is where we split up into two,' he announced. 'We'll meet up in the square in a hour's time.'

They set off with Milton in charge of one group. The dozen or so riders caused some heads to turn as they rode down the main street. They passed the Star Hotel where Milton had happy memories of spending a night. The thought brought another to his mind. It was a thought which so far he had successfully managed to push to the back of his mind, but now it surfaced.

What was going to happen if Erica was dead?

Well, it was in the lap of the gods. Or in God's hands, as the doctor preferred to call it. He himself was an atheist although he had been brought up by the nuns. In fact he had often thought about his lack of religious conviction, even though he had been forced to go to service every day and say his prayers before each meal and before going to bed at night. It was times like this, though, when someone you cared for was at death's door, that brought home to you the possibilities of prayer. Last night, for the first time in years, he had given it serious thought before he had gone to sleep under the stars. He had refrained from praying, but that didn't mean that in future he wouldn't advance his own prayer in the hope that Erica would recover from her gunshot wound.

They arrived at the livery stable. A middle-aged man who had been reading a dime magazine became instantly alert when the group of riders approached.

Milton explained who they were and what they wanted.

'You say he was riding a black stallion?' demanded the keeper of the livery stable.

'That's right. The horse had probably been ridden quite hard.'

'He called here this morning.'

'How long ago?'

'I'd say about three hours.'

So Simms was still the same distance in front of them as when they had started.

'What did he ask for?'

'He wanted the horse fed and watered.'

'What did he do while he was waiting?'

'Nothing. He just sat on the gate eating an apple.'

'When he left, did you notice which way he went?'

'Sure. He went south.'

This confirmed Milton's theory that

Simms was heading for Texas, and then possibly for Mexico. The gunslinger probably had a few thousand dollars to spend, and Mexico had several advantages as a place to spend it. In the first place he wouldn't have to worry about the arm of the law catching up with him for any crimes he had committed, since Mexico had its own legislation. Also the climate was more congenial than the harsh climate here. Yes, Mexico would have a great deal to recommend it, not to mention the wine and *señoritas*.

When they met up with the other group of cowboys he informed them that they were still on Simms's trail, but that the gunslinger was still about three hours ahead of them. If he had thought there would be any suggestion of turning back he was completely reassured by their reply.

'Right, let's go,' said one.

There was a chorus of agreement from the others.

18

Although the posse had met only a few travellers on their way from Cotterton to Adamsville, once they were on their way to the next town, Sula, they met more riders. Milton was able to stop them from time to time and ask whether a man riding a black stallion had been riding towards Sula, the answer was always in the affirmative.

On one occasion they saw a horse-drawn caravan with the words, *Jesus Saves* blazoned on it, which had drawn up at the side of the road. Sitting in the driver's seat was a middle-aged man in preacher's garb. He was a plump man with white whiskers who looked as though he would be happy with a host of small children round him.

'God be with you, young man,' he said, when Milton reined up in front of him.

'And with you, preacher,' said Milton, pleasantly. 'Can you tell me if you've seen a rider on a black stallion heading towards Sula.'

'A rider on a black stallion,' the preacher said, thoughtfully.

At that moment a pretty dark-skinned young woman popped her head out through the flap.

'I saw him, Father,' she stated. 'He passed us when you were having your afternoon nap.'

'Bless my soul, daughter, do you have to tell everyone that I indulge in an afternoon siesta?' he said good-naturedly.

'So you saw him?' asked Milton.

'Yes, he seemed in a hurry.'

'He would be. We're a posse who are hunting him.'

'Then he's an outlaw?' The rest of her body appeared.

'He's wanted for killing three men,' replied Milton.

'What's his name?' enquired the preacher.

'Simms.'

'Then I shall pray for him, tonight, because he is surely on his way to hell if he has killed three men.'

'If he's about three hours in front of you you're not going to stand much chance of catching him,' said his daughter, with annoying practicality.

'We can only hope that he doesn't realize that we are following him, and that he slows down,' said Milton.

'Maybe he'll spend some time in Sula, and you'll be able to catch him there,' she said, thoughtfully.

Some of the cowboys had taken advantage of the temporary halt to have a smoke.

Milton had drawn up his horse near the front of the caravan. He studied the young woman who with her dark skin and thick dark hair looked more like a Mexican than an American.

'Can I ask you a question?'

'Sure.' She flashed him a smile.

'How is it that you are heading for Sula, when all the riders we've met have been heading for Adamsville towards the west?'

'It's simple. We've been running a church in Adamsville. But unfortunately Papa has a bad chest. The doctor advised him to go south where the climate is warmer. So we're heading for Mexico.'

'If my guess is correct that's where Simms is heading for,' stated Milton.

'What's he look like?'

'I never met him. But he shot the lady I was working for and, as I've said, killed three men.'

'He's a thin man, with a thin face,' supplied one of the cowboys, who had overheard the conversation. 'The one distinctive thing about him is that he wears two guns. He boasts that he can draw a gun with his left hand as quickly as he can with his right.'

The young woman shivered. 'He doesn't sound the sort of person I'd ever want to meet.'

'I think the chances are pretty remote,' said Milton, with a smile. The cowboys had finished smoking their cigarettes.

'By the way, what's your name?' the preacher's daughter asked Milton.

'Adam Milton.'

'Well good luck, Adam, on your mission.'

Milton gave her a wave as he led the riders on their way.

'I hope he doesn't catch up with the gunslinger,' she told her father.

'Why not?'

'If the gunslinger is as quick drawing his guns as they say then there will only be one conclusion to a gunfight. Adam Milton will be killed.'

19

When they arrived in Sula the posse again split up in order to go to the livery stables.

'There are three livery stables in the town,' Milton told them.

'So you know Sula?' asked one of the cowboys.

'Yes, I spent some time here,' said Milton, shortly. He didn't explain that he had been a bounty hunter in the town and that he had in fact put two outlaws behind bars in addition to killing two more.

The group of cowboys that Milton was leading called at the nearest livery stable. They soon realized that they had drawn a blank.

'Nobody has called here today to have his horse fed,' said the keeper of the stable.

'Thanks,' said Milton, as he headed

for the town square where he had arranged to meet the others.

The two other groups when they joined him, also reported that the livery stables hadn't seen a rider on a black stallion.

Indecision was in the air. Milton knew he had to make the choice for them.

'Simms could have done either of two things. In the first place he could have carried on riding on his way to Hawkesville. That means he would probably have called at a farm on the way to feed and water his horse.'

'What's the alternative?' demanded a cowboy.

'He could have decided to hole up here. As you've seen, it's a growing town. There are at least a dozen saloons here, there are probably a dozen banks, in addition to a couple of hotels, a theatre and an opera house. He might think this is a good place to go into hiding for a while.'

'So what do we do?' demanded

another cowboy.

'You all go home. You've done more than can be reasonably expected to find Mr Trimble's killer. Not to mention his two sons. You've got to go and help to keep the ranch running.'

'Are you coming with us?' demanded the cowboy.

'No, I've still got some unfinished business.'

Several of them wished him luck before they swung their horses round and headed back towards Adamsville.

Milton remembered from his last visit a saloon in the town called the Duck and Quill. He recalled that it served excellent home-made food. He rode towards it and tied his horse outside.

To his relief the same couple were keeping the saloon. He ordered a pint of beer and a steak. When he was eating his meal the owner's wife came to enquire if it was all right.

'It's as good as it always was,' he replied.

'Well, if it isn't Mr Milton,' she said, when realization dawned. 'We haven't seen you for some time.'

'For too long, Molly' he replied. 'Can you fix me up with a room for the night, I'm tired of sleeping on the hard ground. Oh, and a bath.'

'No problem, Adam,' she replied.

'You remembered my name?'

'I remember most things that go on around here. Some of them aren't even advisable to remember,' she said, enigmatically.

As he was soaking in his tub his mind drifted to the last time he had been in the town, over two years ago. Was the crooked sheriff still in town in his official capacity? True, it had been several months since he had wiped the dust of the town from his feet, but the sheriff had been only middle-aged. He would be expected to carry on in his post for several years. He was the sort of lying, cheating sheriff who survived for years. Come to think of it the sheriff owed him $2,000 for catching the members of the Smollet gang. He had long ago given up any hope of regaining the money. Still it would be interesting to see the sheriff's reaction if he walked into his office and demanded his money.

He smiled at the thought as he ducked his head below the water.

20

When Milton awoke the following morning the first thing he was aware of was the sound of bells. He had lost track of the days, but he correctly concluded that today was Sunday.

After a leisurely breakfast he set out for a just as leisurely stroll around the town. Before he set out he had checked his revolver. There was always the chance that he might come across Simms, and the last thing he would want to do would be to confront him unarmed.

He knew from his past visit that Sula was a growing town. Among its new buildings pride of place had to be given to the opera house. He reached it and stood outside the magnificent edifice, admiring its Gothic columns and water-fountains. His thoughts strayed to his visit to Chicago with Erica. She had asked him to go to the opera with her, but he had refused, saying that he preferred to spend his evening at the boxing-booths. Now he regretted not having gone with her. It would have been a small sacrifice to repay her for taking him to Chicago.

Would he ever see her alive again? The depressing thought persisted as he continued his stroll. Of course there was nothing to stop him from calling off the search for Simms. He could jump on his horse and ride back to Cotterton. That way he could resolve the uncertainty as to whether he would find Erica alive. The only argument against that course of action was that it would leave Simms to carry on living. And he had sworn to Erica that he would catch the bastard, to avenge her shooting. Why did life have to be so complicated?

He was mulling over the decision whether to return to Cotterton or not when he suddenly realized that he had stopped outside a church. The service, instead of being held in the church, was being conducted in the open air. The idea obviously was to attract the interest of passers-by. The idea seemed to have been a success judging by the number who were watching the service.

The churchgoers were singing the popular hymn 'We'll All Gather at the River'. There were a few dozen of them and as Milton idly scanned their faces he was pleasantly surprised to see two that he recognized. It was the preacher and his daughter whom the posse had met when they were on their way to Sula. The preacher's daughter was also looking around at the watchers and she in her turn spotted Milton. She waved to him and indicated that he could join her among the churchgoers. He waved a declining hand in reply.

The atmosphere was pleasant and there were friendly smiles on the faces of many of the watchers. However it came to an abrupt end when a cowboy in the background began to fire his revolver into the air. It became apparent that he was drunk when he slurred his opening sentence.

'Why don't you lot get back in church where you belong?'

The reply came from the preacher Milton had met.

'This is all God's church.' He waved his arms to indicate the whole scene around them.

'Who says so?' said the cowboy, belligerently.

'God says so,' replied the preacher.

'But God's up there, and we're down here,' replied the cowboy.

'If you would care to stay behind after the service, I'll explain how we know all about God's word,' said the preacher.

'I don't want to hear any more,' shouted the cowboy. To emphasize his point he fired a shot over the heads of the churchgoers. There was a collective gasp of horror from them. Some moved further back as though seeking the safety of the church itself.

'That's right, get back in the church

where you belong,' shouted the cowboy, firing another shot over their heads. That this one was lower than the other was illustrated by the fact that it hit one of the bonnets of the ladies. She gave a terrified scream and dived into the safety of the church.

'You'd better put that gun away before you hurt somebody,' said Milton.

The cowboy swung to face him. The gap between them opened up like the parting of the Red Sea.

'Who are you to tell me what to do?' The cowboy's gun was now pointing at Milton.

'You don't want to kill somebody, and then get hanged for it, do you?'

The cowboy's answer was to fire a shot over Milton's head. It didn't miss him by more than a couple of inches.

'If you want to play games, why don't you put that gun back in your holster and we'll see who's the quickest on the draw.'

The cowboy considered the proposal. 'No. I've had a few drinks so you're bound to be quicker than me.'

He turned his attention to the rapidly disappearing crowd.

'That's right. Get back in church where you belong.'

He fired a couple of shots over their heads to hurry them on their way. Soon there was only the preacher whom Milton had met on the trail left outside. The cowboy aimed a shot above his head.

To Milton's horror the shot missed its target. Instead of passing harmlessly above the preacher's head, it hit him in the back. He collapsed in a pool of blood.

Milton's reaction was instinctive. He drew his revolver with startling rapidity and shot the cowboy in the head.

21

An hour or so later Milton found himself in familiar surroundings. He was back in Sula jail.

'Welcome back, Milton,' the sheriff almost purred.

'I shot a guy who had just shot a preacher,' Milton explained.

'It's up to the court to decide whether you're guilty or not. In the meantime, just make yourself comfortable. I've even kept your old cell for you.' The sheriff chuckled as he went back to the outer office.

Milton assessed the situation. His present position would interfere with his plans to catch up with Simms, but there was nothing he could do about it. He didn't regret killing the cowboy. An eye for an eye, said the good book. Well, he had avenged the killing of the preacher. He had no doubt that the trial would be a routine one. He would be released as soon as the evidence was presented. Then that would be that. He would be a free man once again. The one consolation was that this trial wouldn't be rigged the same way as his previous trial. Then he had been accused of being one of the Smollet gang. The number of times he had denied it hadn't made any difference. The sheriff had framed him. The court had believed the sheriff. And therefore he had been sentenced. It was only the fact that Smollet had died while in prison and confessed the truth about him on his deathbed that had caused his release.

On the following day the deputy sheriff announced that he had a visitor.

'It's a young lady,' he added.

It was the preacher's daughter. She was dressed in black.

'I'm so sorry, Adam.' She could hardly hold back the tears.

'I'm not sorry. I mean I'm not sorry I killed him.'

126

'My father would have been proud of the way he died. He had seen that everyone was safe in the church before going in himself.'

'He was a brave man,' said Adam, simply.

'Do you know how long it will be before you will come to trial?'

'It's usually about a week. Wait a minute.' He called the deputy sheriff. 'Can this young lady come into the cell. We can't talk like this between the bars.'

'I'm the daughter of the preacher who was killed,' she explained.

'I suppose it won't do any harm. Especially since the sheriff isn't here,' said the deputy, letting her into the cell.

'There's one thing I'd like to know,' said Milton.

'What's that?'

'I don't know your name. You know mine, but I don't know yours.'

'Rosita.'

'Rosita. That's — unusual.'

'My mother was Mexican. She died about a year ago. We travelled to

Adamstown where father had a church. But lately he'd been suffering with a severe chest complaint. I'd lie awake at night listening to him coughing. That's why we were going back to Mexico. The doctor said the climate might help to cure his chest. I didn't think so though. In my opinion he had only a few months to live at the most. His quick death might have been a providential release.' She choked on the last words. Tears began to roll down her cheeks.

Milton involuntarily took her in his arms. He held her while she sobbed her heart out.

The deputy appeared on the scene.

'Hey! That's not allowed,' he stated.

'She's lost her father.'

'And I'll lose my job if the sheriff comes back and catches you.'

'It's all right, Adam, I'm going,' said Rosita. She kissed him lightly on the cheek before heading out of the jail.

Some time later the sheriff himself put in an appearance.

'I've got news for you,' he told Milton.

'What is it?'

'Your trial is due on Friday.'

'So I've got four more days to spend in this stinking place.'

'I wouldn't count your chickens if I were you. The judge is against all kinds of killing.'

'But the cowboy I killed had already killed a preacher. He could have turned his gun on any of the people who were watching the church service.'

'I don't think it'll cut any ice with him. As I said, he's against any killing. I just thought I'd let you know,' said the sheriff, with a chuckle. As he returned to his office, he called out. 'Happy dreams, Milton.'

22

Rosita was a regular visitor to the jail. She always brought some fruit or tortillas. The only day she failed to turn up was the day when they buried her father.

The following day, Thursday, Milton could see from her face that she had been crying a great deal. The sheriff was away and the deputy was in charge.

'Can you let her in the cell?' asked Milton. 'I promise I won't try to escape. And anyhow the trial is tomorrow. I'll be a free man then.'

'I wouldn't bet on it,' said the deputy enigmatically. Nevertheless he opened the cell door for Rosita to step inside.

'It was a lovely service,' she said, between sobs. 'Father would have been proud of it. The church was full. All the church congregation were there and hundreds of the townsfolk. Many of them had to listen to the service outside. They left the doors open so that they could hear the service.'

Milton put his arms around her to comfort her. He realized, not for the first time, that she was a very shapely young lady. Their faces were close together. There were tears on her eyelashes. She moved closer in his arms. Milton had had enough experience of women to know when one of them was offering her lips to be kissed. They held the position for what seemed ages before Milton eventually drew away.

He correctly read the hurt expression on her face.

'I'm sorry,' he said, inadequately.

'I wasn't asking you to marry me, for God's sake,' she hissed. 'It was just a kiss to show how grateful I've been for the help you've given me these past few days.'

The deputy sheriff, who had arrived to lock the cell up for the night, overheard the remark.

'You didn't do very well there, Milton,' he observed with a chuckle.

★ ★ ★

The day of the trial dawned bright and cloudless. Milton could see enough of the sky beyond the bars of his cell to verify the fact. In a few hours' time I will be able to stroll out there and enjoy the fresh air, he told himself.

After he had shaved and washed the sheriff paid him a rare visit.

'It's good to see that you've smartened yourself up for the trial,' he observed.

'I don't see you doing anything to improve yourself,' retorted Milton. 'Maybe if you lost a few stone it would help.'

The sheriff scowled. The deputy, who had come with him, concealed a grin.

'I've come to advise you that you can have a lawyer, if you need one,' said the sheriff.

'Thanks, but I think I can manage on

my own,' said Milton, drily.

'Suit yourself,' said the sheriff. He turned and headed back towards his office.

'If I were you, I'd have a lawyer,' stated the deputy. 'The judge is a stickler for protocol. If you don't know the correct way to conduct your defence it could count against you.'

Milton hesitated. 'All right,' he said at last. 'Whom do you suggest?'

'There's a young guy who's just setting up as a lawyer. His name is Len Wick. He probably won't charge you anything. He'll be glad of the experience.'

'All right. Will you see that he'll be in court to defend me?'

'Sure,' said the deputy. 'We want this trial to be fair and above board, don't we?'

Milton wasn't sure whether Rosita would visit him after their altercation the day before. To his delight she did turn up.

'Before you say anything,' he said, 'I

wish to apologize for yesterday.'

'There's nothing to apologize for. Maybe I expected too much.'

'I'll make up for it, when I'm released, I promise you.'

'Let's get you released first, then I'll see that you'll keep your promise.'

Because of the presence of the sheriff in his office they were forced to hold their conversation with the cell bars between them. Milton put his hand out through the bars. Rosita recognized the gesture and took hold of his fingers. They stayed like that for several moments while they looked into each other's eyes.

The sheriff came through the door.

'I'm sorry to break up this cosy lovers' meeting, but Milton will be expected in court in half an hour.'

'I'll see you there,' Rosita told Milton, as she waved him a cheerful goodbye.

23

When Milton was led into the court-room he was surprised to see that the room was full. A young man with some prominent pimples on his face stepped forward.

'I'm Len Wick, your lawyer,' he introduced himself.

'Pleased to meet you, Len,' said Milton.

'I just want to give you some advice,' said Len.

'I'm always ready to listen to advice,' replied Milton.

'Well, the judge who will be trying the case is named Judge Foley. He's a stickler for protocol. Just answer his questions and don't advance any opinions unless I say it's all right to do so. Do you understand.'

'Yes, I think I understand,' said Milton, heavily.

'Whatever you do, don't lose your temper.'

'I've got the picture,' said Milton. 'I'll answer the judge's questions and wait for him to say that I've been released.'

At that moment the judge entered. Everyone in the courtroom stood. Judge Foley was a big man who looked every inch a judge from his copious side-whiskers to his stern expression.

After everyone had sat down the clerk of the court announced:

'The case under consideration is the murder of Sol Pope. The person on trial is Adam Milton.'

It was the first time Milton had known that the guy he had killed was named Sol Pope. He wasn't too happy about the case being referred to as murder. After all the guy Sol Pope was the one who had committed a murder. He had shot the preacher in cold blood.

'Who's the prosecuting council?'

'I am, your worship.' An immaculately dressed middle-aged man stepped forward. He wore a dark-grey pin-stripe suit, a shirt which showed the correct amount of white cuff below his sleeves and in his buttonhole he wore a carnation. Milton took an instant dislike to him.

'Right, Mr Crossley, if you will open the case.'

'The case for the prosecution, your worship, is quite straightforward. It is that on Sunday, the eleventh of April, 1884, the defendant, Adam Milton, shot Sol Pope in the side of the head, killing him instantly.'

'He had just killed the preacher, by shooting him in the back,' protested Milton.

'You will not speak unless you are spoken to, Mr Milton,' said the judge, sternly. 'I expect you to control your client, Mr Wick,' he added.

'I'm sorry your honour,' said Wick, contritely. To Milton he whispered. 'Keep quiet, or it could damage your case.'

'Prior to the killing, Sol Pope had shot and killed a preacher named Miles

Winter. I have several witnesses who will testify that Pope was drunk at the time he killed the preacher. He had fired several shots over the heads of the preacher and the rest of the worshippers who were gathered outside the church. As far as Pope was concerned it was merely a bit of fun. Unfortunately it got out of hand.'

'Where was Milton standing while this shooting was going on?'

'He was standing to the side of Mr Pope, about fifty feet away.'

'Were there many other people around where Mr Milton was standing?'

'Yes, from witnesses I have questioned it seems there were about a hundred people outside the church listening to the service.'

'None of them raised a finger when Mr Pope was shot?'

'That's correct, your worship. Now with your permission I'd like to question the defendant.'

'Carry on, Mr Crossley.'

Milton took the oath. The lawyer stood in front of him. He wiped an imaginary speck of dust from his lapel.

'Would you tell the court what is your present occupation?'

'I'm a personal bodyguard to a rancher in Crossville.'

'And before that?'

'I was a bounty hunter.'

'You were a bounty hunter.' The lawyer paused to give the occupation an emphasis. He continued: 'As such you killed several men, I believe.'

'That's right.'

'So you know all about killing men,' he stated thoughtfully.

Milton said nothing.

'Since killing was your profession, you'd know exactly how many bullets a revolver will hold.' What was he driving at?

'Six,' replied Milton, shortly.

'As a bounty hunter it was very important for you to keep a check on the number of bullets in your opponent's gun.'

'Obviously.'

'Then why didn't you count the number of bullets that Mr Pope fired? He had fired all six bullets. He didn't have another bullet left in his gun, yet you shot him in cold blood.'

There was a collective gasp of surprise from the audience at the revelation.

'I didn't count the number of bullets. I had no idea he was going to shoot the preacher.'

'Couldn't you have physically overpowered him? After all you were near enough to him to take the gun away from him.'

'As I said, I didn't count the number of bullets. I thought he could have swung round and started firing into the crowd who were watching him. In which case there could have been more killing.'

'To change the subject, Mr Milton, you claim to be a bounty hunter, but isn't it true that at one time you were a member of the gang of outlaws known as the Smollet gang?'

'It's not true,' yelled Milton. Wick gripped his arm tightly in order to try to stifle any further outburst.

'But you were sentenced to five years' hard labour for being a member of the gang,' said Crossley, smoothly.

'I was framed,' snapped Milton.

'You were framed?' Crossley studied him with his head to one side, his whole attitude conveying disbelief.

'I've got an official pardon to prove it.'

'Where is the pardon now?'

'I left it at the ranch where I was working at Cotterton.'

Suddenly there was a movement in the audience.

'May I say something, your honour?' asked a female voice. It belonged to Rosita.

'Who are you?' demanded Judge Foley.

'My name is Rosita. It was my father who was killed by the cowboy named Sol Pope.'

'Yes, you may take the stand, Miss Winter.'

After being sworn in, Rosita began. 'My father was killed by Sol Pope. He was shot down in cold blood. My father was the loveliest of men. He spent his life working for the church and its people. He didn't deserve to be shot like a dog outside the church which he loved.' She choked back a sob.

'If it's difficult for you to go ahead . . . ' said the judge, sympathetically.

Rosita waved a dismissive hand. 'If I had been standing outside and had had a gun in my hands I would have shot Sol Pope myself for what he did to my father.' There was a loud murmur of agreement from the audience. 'I would personally like to say thank you to Mr Milton for killing Sol Pope before he did any further damage. I don't believe what I'm hearing, that Mr Milton is being accused of murder himself. Mr Milton is a public-spirited person who came to this town as the leader of a posse which was hunting a known killer. Mr Milton should be given a medal for his public spiritedness, instead of being accused of murder.'

From the judge's reaction he was obviously taken aback at the praise of the accused. The reaction of the audience was far more positive. They burst into loud applause.

The judge banged his gavel for silence. When it arrived he cleared his throat. He was obviously going to make an important announcement.

'Taking into account the forthright defence of the accused by Miss Winter, I have to declare that Mr Milton is found not guilty of the unlawful killing of Sol Pope.'

There were several 'hurrahs' from the audience.

'There is only one further stipulation,' said the judge. 'The court must see a copy of the pardon Mr Milton received after his last sentence was terminated. He will therefore remain in custody until it is produced.'

'What do I do now?' Milton asked the deputy sheriff, as he was being led out of the court.

'Give me the address of the ranch where you worked. I'll send a telegram. They can post the pardon to us. After we've examined it, you'll be a free man.'

'But that could take another four or five days,' Milton groaned.

'You have to thank the young lady that you aren't spending longer than that in prison,' retorted the deputy.

24

Rosita came to visit him every day. The first occasion was a difficult one for Milton. It was made doubly difficult by the fact that the sheriff was in the outer office and so was overhearing their conversation.

'I can't thank you enough for your speech,' he said. 'I don't know whether I deserved it all, though.'

'Of course you did,' she retorted. 'You deserved every word.'

Somehow her hand rested on one of the iron bars of the cell. It seemed only natural for Milton's hand to rest lightly on hers. She smiled the secret smile which women often resort to in such circumstances.

'How long will it be before the pardon will arrive?'

'Probably about five days.'

'Then I suppose you'll be going

back to Cotterton.'

'I've got to find out what happened to Miss Chambers. Whether she's alive or dead.'

'I hope for your sake she's alive.'

Milton glanced at her with surprise. In the semi-darkness of the cells it was difficult fully to gauge her expression.

'Why do you say that?'

'Because if she's dead you'll never forgive yourself for not guarding her properly. You told me how you went on a wild-goose chase and left her alone. Then when you returned she had been shot.'

'We'll just have to wait and see, won't we.'

The sheriff announced that Rosita's time was up. She held Milton's hand for a moment. Then she kissed his fingers.

'Life is never easy, Milton,' she stated. 'Nor love,' she added, before going out through the door.

★ ★ ★

The pardon arrived five days later as the deputy had prophesied. It was in the early evening when the deputy brought it in.

'I've got good news and bad news,' he stated.

'I'll have the good news first. I haven't had much lately.'

'I've got the pardon here. I've shown it to the clerk of the court. You're free to go.'

'What's the bad news?' enquired Milton, as he pocketed the pardon.

'I sent the telegram to the ranch where you worked. The housekeeper sent the reply. He added that your employer, Miss . . . '

'Chambers is dead.'

The news hit Milton like a thunderbolt. Somehow he had been so sure that she would hang on to life.

He left the prison in a daze. He found Rosita's caravan where she told him it would be parked. As he approached she saw at once from his face that something was amiss.

'For a man who's just come out of prison, you don't seem very pleased about it.'

'I've just received bad news.'

'It's about Miss Chambers, isn't it,' she said, with sudden insight.

'Yes, she's dead.' Although the words sounded casual, emotion was etched in the tight lines of his face.

'Come into the caravan.'

She led him inside. Most of the space inside was taken up by a bed.

'Lie down,' she commanded. He did so, after having taken off his jacket and shoes.

'Turn over.'

He did so. She began to massage his shoulders. It was an extremely pleasant sensation. At first her fingers pressed lightly into his flesh, then gradually her pressure became firmer. At one stage she told him to take off his shirt. He complied: This gave her more opportunity to massage his back.

The tension which had built up in the jail was gradually slipping away. He began to breathe deeply. Her fingers became more probing. The only thing on his mind was this extremely pleasant sensation. He was aware of noises outside. A cart passed by and he could hear the jingle of the horses' bridles.

'Mm, this is lovely,' he stated.

'Did you know your muscles were as stiff as this?'

'I've never thought about it.'

'Just close your eyes and relax.'

He did as she commanded and in no time he was asleep. Darkness was now beginning to edge in. Rosita fetched a blanket and placed it carefully over him.

When Milton awoke the dawn chorus was beginning to make itself heard. He opened his eyes and it took him a few seconds to realize where he was. He was obviously in a strange bed with an unexpected companion lying close to him. In the half-light he could partly distinguish Rosita's face. She was fast asleep and her black hair had tumbled over her face. He leaned on one elbow.

He began to push her hair away gently from her face.

She opened her eyes. 'What are you doing?' she asked.

'I'm moving your hair so that I can kiss you.'

'You didn't want to kiss me the last time I gave you the chance.'

'I've realized since then what a fool I've been.'

Their faces were closer together. They held the pose like two people waiting to have their photographs taken. At last she said:

'If you're sure you're doing the right thing . . . '

'I've never been more sure,' he said, as his lips found hers.

Eventually she drew away. 'You've got some unfinished business to see to.'

'The business can wait,' he said, as he tried to kiss her again.

She slipped off the bed. 'It's got to be sorted out first.'

'I suppose you're right,' he said, regretfully.

'You know I am. Now I'll make breakfast while you dress. Then you'll be able to make an early start.'

After they had eaten the breakfast of beans and bacon which she had prepared Milton asked:

'What do you intend to do now?'

'I've got some work to do here.'

'What kind of work?'

'The church my father was working for has said they would like to lay a commemoration stone on the spot where he was shot. They asked me if I could help to collect some of the money from the members. It will mean going round their houses to collect it.'

'Do you mind doing it?'

'No, it will give me something to do.'

'So you'll be staying in Sula?'

'For a couple of weeks at least — until the stone is laid.'

'That means I'll know where to get in touch with you.'

'Are you sure you'll want to?'

'There's only one answer to that. Come here.'

She moved close to him. He kissed her. This time the kiss seemed to go on for ever.

25

The following day Milton arrived back in Cotterton. As he rode up to the ranch he saw that the blinds on the windows were drawn. He thought that it was like the closing of a chapter of his life. There were a few things to attend to here, then he would be on his way back to Rosita. It was fortunate in a way that no personal feelings had begun between himself and Erica. Not that he had had any chance of being more than just a good friend to the lady owner of the ranch.

Calan and Mars were on the gate as usual. Milton dismounted.

'When was the funeral?' he demanded.

'The day before yesterday,' said Calan.

'You didn't get the guy who shot Mr Trimble and his sons?' demanded Mars.

Milton shook his head. 'Not yet.'

'Are you going back to try to get him?' demanded Mars.

'It's unfinished business,' replied Milton.

'Well, there's more unfinished business inside,' said Calan. 'The lawyer from Chicago was at Miss Chambers' funeral. He said he wanted to see you.'

The housekeeper, when Milton went inside the house, repeated the statement.

'I wonder what he wants to see me about?' asked a puzzled Milton.

'I don't know. He didn't say.'

'Tell me what happened — in the end.'

'Miss Chambers never recovered consciousness. The doctor said the bullet had lodged in her spine. If she had ever recovered consciousness she would never have been able to walk again. She would have been a cripple for the rest of her life.'

'The bastard.' Milton was pacing up and down the room slamming his fist into his hand. 'And to think that the bastard is still a free man.'

'It was a lovely funeral,' continued the housekeeper. 'I think all of Cotterton were there.'

'I'll go to see her grave before I leave,' said Milton.

'There are some flowers in the garden behind the house. You can pick some of them to take with you.'

The journey to the cemetery proved to be more emotional than Milton had expected. When he stood at the simple cross which stated: Erica Chambers 1854–1884, he felt tears welling up in his eyes. He brushed them away impatiently.

What a waste of a life. To be gunned down by a gunslinger — and for what? So that old man Trimble could control the two ranches. Well justice had been done there since neither Trimble nor either of his sons would now control the Big C ranch. Yes, justice had been done, the only regret was that the person who had been responsible for all the killings was still at large.

As he stared at the freshly dug earth he repeated the promise he had made when she was still alive. *I'll get the bastard, I swear it. Even if it takes the rest of my life.*

He walked slowly from the grave. He had one more visit to make before he left the big C ranch. He had to pay a visit to the lawyer in Chicago.

★　★　★

The journey was uneventful. From time to time he remembered the last time he had made the journey with Erica by his side. The expression of sadness on his face quashed any inclination among the passengers to speak to him on the journey. In fact, although he never realized it, nobody spoke to him during the whole journey to Chicago.

He arrived in the late afternoon. On his previous visit he had accompanied Erica to the lawyer's office and so he knew exactly where to go. On that occasion he had waited in the coffee shop across the road while Erica concluded her business. He had only come into the waiting room when the half-hour which Erica had told him to wait had ended.

This time, when he announced his name to the clerk he wasn't kept waiting for more than a few minutes.

'Mr Steckley will see you now,' announced the clerk.

Milton went into a comfortably furnished office. Milton had briefly seen Mr Steckley when he had been showing Erica out of his office on the previous occasion. He was a large man with a broken nose which hadn't been set properly, who looked as though he would not have been out of place in the boxing-ring.

'Sit down, Mr Milton,' he said, after shaking hands. When Milton was seated he asked: 'Would you like a drink? Whiskey, perhaps?'

In fact Milton was feeling rather dry after his long journey.

'A whiskey would be fine.'

The lawyer poured two generous glassfuls.

'Of course we were all deeply shocked to hear about Miss Chambers's murder,' he said. He handed Milton his glass.

'It was a shock to us all. The murderer is still at large.'

The lawyer studied Milton as he sipped his whiskey. Eventually he said: 'I've got one more shock for you. Miss Chambers left the Big C ranch to you in her will. You are now the owner of the ranch and all the stock. You are a very rich man indeed, Mr Milton.'

★ ★ ★

Half an hour later Milton knocked at the door of Aunt Emma's cottage. The maid opened the door and led Milton into the parlour. Aunt Emma looked up from the book she was reading.

'I knew you'd come,' she said, as she gave him her hand.

'Why?' he demanded, as he sat down. 'Why did she leave everything to you? Because she trusted you. And because she was partially in love with you, although she didn't know it herself.'

'That's nonsense,' protested Milton, hotly.

'It is? Well, maybe since I'm an old person I'm looking into an imaginary crystal ball too much these days. You'll stay to tea?'

Milton stayed to tea. When it was time to leave she said:

'We'll probably never meet again. There's only one thing I would ask of you: keep the ranch as she would have liked it kept. That way you can keep alive her memory.'

Milton spent the journey back to Cotterton as though he was in a dream. He was the owner of the largest ranch in Cotterton with 2,000 head of cattle. He was rich. The lawyer had said he could have access to the money in Erica's account as soon as he went to see a lawyer in Cotterton. This lawyer, a man named Blindley who worked in conjunction with Mr Steckley, would see that the money in Erica's account in the bank would be transferred to him. Mr Steckley had casually mentioned that it was probably about $10,000.

The only stipulation in the will was that he would maintain the ranch as a going concern. It meant that he could not sell everything and move away with the proceeds. If he did sell up then the escape clause in the will would come into force. The effect of that would be that Milton would forfeit all the proceeds of the sale and the money would all go to various charities. Well, he had no intention of ever selling up. He would be quite happy to run the ranch as Erica would have wished. He couldn't wait to get back to the ranch. *His* ranch. He was sure that the travellers in the stage would wonder at the expression on his face. Fortunately none of them had been travelling on the stage when it left Cotterton two days before and so couldn't assess the difference between the sad-faced young man and this young traveller whose face now wore an expression of delight.

26

When Milton broke the news to Calan and Mars they received it with apparent lack of interest.

'Does that mean we'll be staying on at the ranch?' demanded Mars.

'Sure. Nothing's going to change.'

When he told the housekeeper she was more forthcoming.

'I'm very pleased for you, Mr Milton. I'm sure Miss Chambers made the right choice.'

After having a meal Milton asked the housekeeper for the keys to Erica's desk. He took up the unusual position for him behind the desk and began to go through the papers and bills. They were all neatly arranged in date order. Most of them were of little interest to him. One, however, did catch his eye. He whistled out loud as its implication sunk in.

His first task the following morning was to search out Calan and Mars from the bunkhouse. Some of the cowboys were still there and they offered him their congratulations.

'I can assure you that nothing is going to change,' he stated.

Many of them received the information with relief. Back in his study he put a proposition before Calan and Mars. At first they viewed it with suspicion, then gradually their attitude changed. Eventually they came to an agreement.

He rode into Cotterton where his first call was to see the lawyer. He was a plump, middle-aged man who reminded Milton of Rosita's father. He pushed the thought aside as he accepted the chair he had been offered.

'Would you like a whiskey, Mr Milton?' asked Mr Blindley.

'I'm afraid it's too early in the day for me.'

The lawyer reluctantly put the bottle aside. 'Now what can I do for you?'

'I believe Mr Steckley in Chicago has

been in touch with you.'

'That's right. He sent me a telegram and confirmed it with a letter. The upshot is that you have inherited the entire estate of the late Miss Chambers.'

'He said that you would give me a letter to take to the bank which would give me access to Miss Chambers' account.'

'That's right. I will write it now if you would like to wait.'

'I'll call back for it in, say, half an hour. There's one other matter I would like cleared up.'

'If I can help you, I certainly will.'

'I went through Miss Chambers' files last night and I found that she and one other person were responsible for hiring and paying for the sheriff of the town.'

'That's quite true. Miss Chambers and Mr Trimble paid the sheriff's salary between them.'

'What happens at present, since I believe Mr Trimble's estate hasn't been settled?'

'The sole responsibility will fall on you — until, of course, the Trimble estate is settled. Which could take months.'

'Thank you. That's what I wanted to hear,' said Milton, with a smile.

He seems happy, thought Blindley, as he watched Milton leave. Then, who wouldn't be, having inherited the fortune he has just come into, he added, as he poured himself a whiskey.

Milton's next call was the sheriff's office. He breezed in without knocking.

'Remember me,' he said, taking a seat without being invited.

'Wha — at are you doing, barging into my office like this?' blustered the sheriff.

'I'm the person who you sent on a wild-goose chase to Masonville so that you could get me out of the way while Mr Trimble arranged to have Miss Chambers killed.' Milton delivered the accusation casually, but there no mistaking the threat behind his words.

'I didn't do it. It's a lie. You'll never

be able to prove it,' the sheriff gasped. The panic showed in his terrified face as he held on tightly to the arms of his chair.

'You're quite right, I'll never be able to prove it.'

The sheriff breathed an audible sigh of relief.

'But there is another way in which I can even up the score. You see I've inherited all Miss Chambers' estate.' He tossed the letter confirming this on to the sheriff's desk.

The sheriff scanned it at first with incredulity then with concern as he finished reading it.

'This can't be true.'

'Oh, it is. The will is safe in the hands of the lawyer in Chicago. But now we come to the interesting part. I am now legally your boss.'

'Oh, no you're not.' The sheriff's eyes narrowed craftily. 'I was employed jointly by Miss Chambers and Mr Trimble.'

'Exactly. And since Mr Trimble's

estate hasn't been settled, and probably won't be for several months, it means that I am your sole boss. I checked with Mr Blindley before coming here. It's a nice piece of irony that if you hadn't been behind the scheme to get rid of Miss Chambers, the killer Simms would never have come here and Mr Trimble would probably still be alive.'

'You can't prove anything.' The sheriff seemed to find comfort in restating the situation.

'I agree that there's nothing I can do about that. On the other hand, since I'm your boss, there is something I can do.'

'I suppose it means you're not going to pay me,' said the sheriff, with a scowl.

'More than that, I'm going to sack you.'

'You can't do that.' Panic made him stand up. 'I'm an old man. What will I do?'

'That's your problem. You're sacked as from this moment.'

'I suppose you think you're a big man, sacking me like this.'

'Oh, I haven't finished with you yet. I saw your name in Miss Chambers' accounts. She kept her accounts very carefully — in fact she bought all your clothes. I therefore want all your clothes back. Your jacket. Your boots and your trousers. I'll let you keep your pants on.'

'No. No.' screamed the sheriff. 'You can't do this to me.'

'I can. And if you don't hurry up, I'll take them off you myself.'

The sheriff was sobbing as he took off his boots and trousers.

'Yes, that will do.' Milton surveyed the pathetic figure who was standing in front of him. He felt no pity. This was the weasel who had been behind the scheme to get rid of Erica.

'I want you out of this town. And you'll never set foot in it again. Do you understand?'

The sheriff was sobbing so much that he could only nod.

'Ah, here are your replacements,' said Milton, as Mars and Calan arrived. They were in time to see Milton aiming a kick at the sheriff's ample backside as the lawman stumbled down the street.

27

When he arrived back at the ranch he was met by the housekeeper.

'A telegram has arrived for you,' she informed him.

He hastily opened it. It was from Rosita. It said simply: SIMMS IS IN TOWN.

'I'll be away for a few days,' he told a startled housekeeper, as he raced up the stairs. 'Will you pack some food for me?'

He had tossed the telegram on the table. The housekeeper stole a glance at it.

'I hope you get the bastard,' she said.

Milton arrived in Sula the following day. He had ridden through much of the night, pausing only when the clouds had covered the moon and therefore had called a halt to his progress. He arrived at Rosita's caravan before midday.

Much to his annoyance she wasn't there. He hesitated while he decided what his next step would be.

He obviously had to wait for her to turn up. He tied his horse to the caravan shafts. He knew where she kept the key to the caravan. After a moment's hesitation he reached down under the caravan and found it where it was hooked on a nail.

He opened the door and stepped inside. The bed looked inviting since he had had only a couple of hours sleep on his journey there. He kicked off his boots and lay down. In a less than a minute he was fast asleep.

He was awakened by someone digging him in the ribs and a female voice which he recognized.

'Who's been sleeping in my bed?' the voice was saying.

He opened his eyes. Rosita was standing above the bed. He opened his arms in a universally recognized invitation. She came to lie by his side. Their kiss went on and on.

Eventually she broke away.

'How long have you been here?' she asked.

'A couple of hours maybe. Where will I find Simms?'

'He's in a saloon every afternoon. It's called the Golden Goose. I saw him by accident when I was out collecting for the church. He's as you described him and he wears two guns. You can see the bulges under his coat.'

'Well done. So all I've got to do is to go to the Golden Goose and kill him.' There was a hardness in his voice which she hadn't come across before. She shivered involuntarily.

'Don't go, Adam,' she pleaded. 'He'll kill you. Oh, my God, what have I done by telling you this?'

'You've helped me avenge the killings of Miss Chambers and three others. Don't worry about me. I know how to take care of myself. Just cook me a celebration meal when I get back.'

Rosita's answer was to strip off her

shirt. Milton could see her beautiful breasts.

'Stay with me, Adam.' She moved close to him. 'Let the law take care of Simms.'

He knew what she was offering. The temptation was almost too much. He could feel her warm skin against him. It would be so easy to take her in his arms and accept what she was giving him.

With a determined mental effort he moved away from her. He stood up, carefully avoiding looking in her direction. He checked his gun. He heard her movement as she slipped her shirt back on. He knew she was standing behind him.

He turned.

'When I come back, I want everything to be right in the eyes of the church.'

'God bless you, Adam,' she whispered, as he turned to leave the caravan.

He went out in the late afternoon sun. He remembered the Golden

Goose saloon from his previous stay in Sula. He walked steadily toward it. He had emptied his mind of all thoughts about Erica and Rosita. He knew from past experience that he could only succeed in his task if he had a clear mind. It had to be one hundred per cent focused on the task in hand. If it wasn't then the corpse lying on the floor would be his.

The saloon was now about a hundred yards ahead. There were people on the sidewalk but he had chosen to walk in the road. The last thing he wanted was to give way to some mother or other who had been collecting her child from school. It was vital that he kept his concentration. There were no horses to impede his deliberate progress.

Fifty yards to go. It was essential that he thought of Simms merely as another one of his intended victims. The same as he had when he had killed the others when he had been a bounty hunter. If he started thinking of the killer in any other way he would allow emotion to get in the way of his intended killing. He knew that would be fatal.

He arrived at the saloon. He went through the swing-door without hesitating. There was a card-school in the corner. They were concentrating completely on their game and paid no attention to the newcomer. It was not difficult to spot Simms with the two bulges beneath his coat. Milton walked up to the table.

'Mr Simms, I presume,' he said.

Simms's reaction was instantaneous — he went for his guns. Milton's movement, however, was quicker. He hit him on the jaw.

He caught the outlaw as he was about to fall on the floor. He took Simms's two guns and tossed them to the barman.

'Keep these,' he said. 'This guy is wanted for four killings in Cotterton.'

He took off Simms's belt and tied his hands behind his back with it. By now Simms was starting to come around. Milton slung him over his shoulder.

'We're going to see the sheriff,' he informed the now fully conscious outlaw.

As the strange sight moved towards the sheriff's office they caused a stir among the people on the sidewalk. Women stopped and stared. If they had children with them they made sure that they took hold of their children's hands as though Milton and his unwilling companion presented them with some threat. Some of the men on the sidewalk speculated about the reason for the strange sight, but mostly they accepted it philosophically. After all this was the West and stranger things than this had happened from time to time.

Milton arrived in the sheriff's office. The sheriff and his deputy looked up with stunned surprise when Milton deposited Simms on the floor of the office.

'This is the guy who killed four people in Cotterton,' he stated. 'When he comes for trial I can have a score of witnesses to find him guilty and then see him hanged.'

'So this is Simms,' said the sheriff. He was already visualizing a big trial with himself as the central witness. He'd play down the part this thorn in the flesh, Milton, had played in capturing the outlaw. Yes. It would be his trial and he would reap the glory from it.

He dragged Simms back up on to his feet.

'I'm afraid you'll be spending some time in our company,' he said, as he led the outlaw towards a cell.

He pushed him inside and was about to lock the door when Simms spoke.

'Can't you take this belt off me?'

The sheriff, seeing no danger in the innocent request, untied it. Simms reacted like lightning. He slid a knife from a holster under his shirt and stabbed the sheriff in the heart. It took Milton a split second to spot what Simms's next move would be. The outlaw went for the sheriff's gun as the lawman began to fall. Milton also drew his gun. To the startled watching deputy there was little to judge between the speed of the reactions of the two men. But Milton was a fraction of a second quicker. It showed in the way he began to pump bullets in the outlaw.

★ ★ ★

Rosita was waiting for him on the top of the caravan steps. When she saw him in the distance she raced towards him.

'Are you all right?' she demanded, as she flung herself into his arms.

'Yes, I'm all right.'

'Thank God.'

'Simms and the sheriff are dead. I'll tell you about it when we're having that dinner you're going to cook for me.'

Later, he described the events.

'There was one thing that warned me that Simms could be planning something,' he concluded. 'He didn't move when I carried him to the sheriff's office. I would have expected him to struggle. Or at least to swear, but he was completely calm, as though he was planning something.'

Afterwards, when night was drawing in, Rosita asked:

'What are you going to do tomorrow?'

'I'm going to get married, of course.'

The pause at the end of the statement went on for so long that Milton wondered whether she had heard it.

Eventually Rosita said: 'Who to?'

'To you, of course. If you'll have me.'

'You know I will,' she said, as she snuggled up to him on the bed.

They were married in the church where Rosita's father had been killed. It wasn't the following day, in fact it was three days later, since Rosita had insisted on buying a white wedding-dress for the occasion. To complete the occasion Milton bought her a wedding ring.

'Are you sure you can afford that?' demanded a concerned Rosita when she saw the price of the ring.

'No problem. I came into some money,' said Milton, casually.

The wedding itself was a moving ceremony.

Most of the church congregation seemed to be there. Rosita struggled to control her emotions, but the thought that her father wasn't on hand to give her away proved too much for her. She burst into tears. The preacher led her into the vestry so that she could recover her composure.

Afterwards she asked Milton: 'What do we do now?'

'We do what married couples do, then we'll take the caravan back to Cotterton.'

They eventually arrived in Cotterton.

'We could have been here quicker if you hadn't kept on going to bed,' said Rosita.

Milton aimed a playful blow at her which she ducked to avoid.

They drove up to the gate. Milton unhitched the horse and tied him to the rail. Rosita was looking around.

'So this is where you work. I'm impressed.'

Milton led her to the front door. He pushed it open. To Rosita's surprise he picked her up.

'Hey! Put me down,' she protested. 'You only carry the bride over the threshold of your own house.'

'I forgot to tell you. This is my house.'

He carried a stunned Rosita inside. The housekeeper came to meet them. Milton introduced them.

'I'm glad to see you've found a bride. It's something that's been missing in this house for years.'

Rosita was still in Milton's arms.

'I'll take this upstairs,' he informed the housekeeper. 'We still have some unfinished business.'

We do hope that you have enjoyed reading this large print book.

Did you know that all of our titles are available for purchase?

We publish a wide range of high quality large print books including:
Romances, Mysteries, Classics
General Fiction
Non Fiction and Westerns

Special interest titles available in large print are:
The Little Oxford Dictionary
Music Book, Song Book
Hymn Book, Service Book

Also available from us courtesy of Oxford University Press:
Young Readers' Dictionary
(large print edition)
Young Readers' Thesaurus
(large print edition)

For further information or a free brochure, please contact us at:
Ulverscroft Large Print Books Ltd.,
The Green, Bradgate Road, Anstey,
Leicester, LE7 7FU, England.
Tel: (00 44) **0116 236 4325**
Fax: (00 44) **0116 234 0205**

Other titles in the
Linford Western Library:

ROPE JUSTICE

Ben Coady

Dan Brady is resting at a creek when, hearing a commotion on the opposite side of the water, he discovers a lynching in progress. Brady's sense of justice spurs him to prevent the lynching. But he finds he's pitched himself into a bitter feud. Now he is faced with a powerful rancher as his enemy, a crooked marshal, a bevy of hard cases and a gunfighter . . . A veteran of many tight spots, Brady might be making his final stand.

GOLD OF THE BAR 10

Boyd Cassidy

Gene Adams and his riders of the Bar 10 had brought in a herd of steers and been paid. Deciding to visit friends, Adams, Tomahawk, Johnny Puma and Red Hawke retrace an old trail on their way back to Texas. But an outlaw gang trails them, interested in the gold in Adams' saddlebags. And ahead of them two killers have kidnapped Johnny's sweetheart, Nancy . . . Can these legendary riders survive the dangers looming on all sides?